HE DROPPED LIGHTLY TO THE ROOF OF THE OLD MILL.
*The Secret of the Old Mill.*          *Frontispiece* (*Page* 183)

# THE HARDY BOYS
# THE SECRET
# OF THE OLD MILL

By
## FRANKLIN W. DIXON
AUTHOR OF
THE HARDY BOYS: THE TOWER TREASURE
THE HARDY BOYS: THE HOUSE ON THE CLIFF

*ILLUSTRATED BY*
## WALTER S. ROGERS

*WITH AN INTRODUCTION BY*
## WILLIAM TAPPLY

## FACSIMILE EDITION

1991
BEDFORD, MA
## APPLEWOOD BOOKS

For further information about these editions, please write: Applewood Books, Box 365, Bedford, MA 01730.

LIBRARY OF CONGRESS CATALOGING-IN-PUBLICATION DATA
Dixon, Franklin W.
     The secret of the old mill / by Franklin W. Dixon;
illustrated by Walter S. Rogers; with an introduction by
William Tapply.—Facsimile ed.
     p.     cm.     —(The Hardy Boys mystery stories)
     At head of title: The Hardy boys.
     Summary: Teenage detectives Frank and Joe Hardy
investigate a case of counterfeiting.
     ISBN 1-55709-146-3
     [1. Mystery and detective stories.  2. Counterfeits and
counterfeiting—Fiction.]     I. Rogers, Walter S., ill.
II. Title.     III. Title: Hardy boys.     IV. Series: Dixon,
Franklin W.  Hardy boys mystery stories.
PZ7.D644Se     1991
[Fic]–DC20                                      91-46349
                                                CIP
                                                AC

10 9 8 7 6 5

# PUBLISHER'S NOTE

Applewood Books is pleased to reissue the original Hardy Boys and Nancy Drew books, just as they were originally published—the Hardy Boys in 1927 and Nancy Drew in 1930. In 1959, the books were condensed and rewritten, and since then, the original editions have been out of print.

Much has changed in America since the books were first issued. The modern reader may be delighted with the warmth and exactness of the language, the wholesome innocence of the characters, their engagement with the natural world, or the nonstop action without the use of violence; but just as well, the modern reader may be extremely uncomfortable with the racial and social stereotyping, the roles women play in these books, or the use of phrases or situations which may conjure up some response in the modern reader that was not felt by the reader of the times.

For good or bad, we Americans have changed quite a bit since these books were first issued. Many readers will remember these editions with great affection and will be delighted with their return; others will wonder why we just don't let them disappear. These books are part of our heritage. They are a window on our real past. For that reason, except for the addition of this note and the introduction by William Tapply, we are presenting *The Secret of the Old Mill* unedited and unchanged from its first edition.

Applewood Books
September 1991

# MY REAL HERO

### By

## WILLIAM TAPPLY

AUTHOR OF
THE BRADY COYNE MYSTERY SERIES: THE SPOTTED CATS
THE BRADY COYNE MYSTERY SERIES: CLIENT PRIVILEGE
THE BRADY COYNE MYSTERY SERIES: DEAD WINTER
& OTHERS

THE QUESTION most frequently asked of us mystery writers is: Where do you get your ideas?

We smile, we shrug, we flap out hands in the air. It's a mystery.

The next most common question I hear is: What writers have influenced you?

That I can answer with more confidence. Dickens, Twain, Dostoyevsky, Dixon, Chandler, Hammett. Wonderful storytellers.

A frown. Dixon?

Of course. Franklin W. Dixon. Very prolific. He wrote all those Hardy Boys books.

It's a joke, of course. There was no Franklin W. Dixon. That was the collective name given to the Stratemeyer Syndicate's stable of writers-for-hire who since the 1920s have created dozens of adventures for

Frank and Joe Hardy, one after the other.

As a boy in the early 1950s I devoured those tales. In that time ATV (Ante television), every kid in my neighborhood collected Hardy Boys books. The brothers were our heroes. Clean-cut, courageous, honest, and fair, they were worthy of our emulation. They represented the values of that uncomplicated time when right was right and wrong was wrong and everybody knew the difference, when virtue was always rewarded and crime never paid, when family was sacred and communities cooperated, and when the American dream still lived, at least in the hearts of young readers.

But my real hero was Franklin W. Dixon. He hooked me on the first page, and he seduced me into the same kind of high-spirited youthful disobedience that he might have allowed Frank and Joe themselves. After my mother ordered lights out, I dived under the covers with my flashlight and my latest Dixon adventure. I always *intended* just to finish the chapter. But he had this trick of ending a chapter in just the place where you had to read on. You couldn't leave Joe sweeping down the river to his certain death. You couldn't stop reading when the brothers were lost at sea or when a desperate criminal was pointing a revolver at the boys or when our heroes were trapped with the counterfeiting gang in a room with no escape.

A Hardy Boys adventure had to be read all at once. I was fully aware that Franklin W. Dixon was manipulating me. I loved it. How marvelous to be able to write a book that did that!

For me—and for all the boys of my generation—Hardy Boys books were our introduction to the mystery/suspense genre. Of course, times—or at least our understanding of the times—have changed. The black-and-white world has become gray, unquestioned values have come under attack, and as often as not, crime pays handsomely.

But the standards by which thrillers are judged remain constant. We still want characters we can admire but who are not bigger than life. We want to share their outrage at crimes against the innocent. We want to believe in their quest. We want to see them endangered. We know what combination of luck and pluck will pull them through. And we want, in the end, to see justice done.

These criteria were imprinted on my young mind, and a quarter of a century later, when I invented Brady Coyne and began to think up adventures for him—and folks began to ask what writers had influenced me—I remembered my hero, Franklin W. Dixon.

And now, thanks to Applewood Books, the Hardy Boys are back. Their adventures can be read, if you choose, as quaint reminders of an America that no longer exists, a time before television and video games and computers, a time before international terrorists and environmental time bombs and nuclear nightmares, a time, if we were to take the books literally, before premarital sex and dysfunctional families and racial strife, before drugs and alcohol and pornography.

Or they can be read as models of well-crafted adventure fiction, and if the plots are a bit formulaic and the outcomes predictable, blame our jaded contemporary sophistication. But don't blame Franklin W. Dixon.

As for me, I'm planning to crawl under the covers with a flashlight and *The Secret of the Old Mill*. I'll be out when I've finished.

# THE HARDY BOYS

# THE SECRET OF THE OLD MILL

By

## FRANKLIN W. DIXON

AUTHOR OF

THE HARDY BOYS: THE TOWER TREASURE
THE HARDY BOYS: THE HOUSE ON THE CLIFF

*ILLUSTRATED BY*

WALTER S. ROGERS

NEW YORK
GROSSET & DUNLAP
PUBLISHERS

Made in the United States of America

# MYSTERY STORIES FOR BOYS

### By FRANKLIN W. DIXON

THE HARDY BOYS: THE TOWER TREASURE

THE HARDY BOYS: THE HOUSE ON THE CLIFF

THE HARDY BOYS: THE SECRET OF THE OLD MILL

(Other Volumes in Preparation)

GROSSET & DUNLAP, PUBLISHERS, NEW YORK

# CONTENTS

iv Contents

# THE HARDY BOYS

# THE SECRET OF THE OLD MILL

## CHAPTER I

### A FIVE DOLLAR BILL

THE afternoon express from the north steamed into the Bayport station to the usual accompanying uproar of clanging bells from the lunch room, shouting redcaps, and a bellowing train announcer.

Among the jostling, hurrying crowd on the platform were two pleasant-featured youths who scanned the passing coaches expectantly.

"I don't see him," said Frank Hardy, the older of the pair, as he watched the passengers descending from one of the Pullman coaches.

"Perhaps he stopped at some other town and intends coming in on the local. It's only an hour later," suggested his brother Joe.

The boys waited. They had met the train expecting to greet their father, Fenton Hardy, the nationally famous detective, who had been away from home for the past two weeks on a

1

murder case in New York. It appeared that they were to be disappointed. When the last of the Bayport passengers had left the train Fenton Hardy was not among them.

"We'll come back and meet the local," said Frank at last.

The brothers were about to turn away and retrace their steps down the platform when they saw a tall, well-dressed stranger swing himself down from the steps of the nearest coach. He was a man of about thirty, dark and clean-shaven, and he hastened over toward them.

"I want to pay a fellow a dollar out of this five," remarked the stranger, as he came up to the boys. "Can you change the bill?"

At the same time he produced a five dollar bill from his pocket and held it out inquiringly.

He was a pleasant-spoken young man and he was evidently in a hurry.

"I could try the lunch room, I suppose, but there's such a crowd that I'll have trouble being waited on," he explained, the bill fluttering in his hands.

Frank looked at his brother and began feeling in his pockets.

"I've got three dollars, Joe. How about you?"

Joe dug up the loose change in his possession. There was a dollar bill, a fifty-cent piece and three quarters.

"Two dollars and a quarter," he announced. "I guess we can make it."

He handed over two dollars to Frank, who added it to the three dollars of his own and gave the money to the stranger, who gave Frank the five dollar bill in exchange.

"Thanks, ever so much," said the young man. "You've saved me a lot of trouble. My friend is getting off at this station and I wanted to give him the dollar before he left. Thanks."

"Don't mention it," replied Frank carelessly, putting the bill in his pocket. "We'll get it changed between us."

The young man nodded, smiled at them and hastened back up the steps of the coach, with a carefree wave of his hand.

"I'm glad we were able to help him out," observed Joe. "It was just by chance that I had that small change too. Mother gave me some money to buy some pie-plates."

"Pie-plates!" exclaimed Frank, with a grin. "There's nothing I'd rather see coming into the house than more pie-plates. More pie-plates mean more pie."

"We might as well go down and get them now, before I forget. There's a shop down the street and we can get the plates and get this five dollar bill changed. It'll help kill time before the local comes in."

The two lads went down the platform, out through the station to the main street of Bayport, basking in the summer sunlight. They were healthy, normal American boys of high school age. Frank, being a year older than his brother, was slightly taller. He was slim and dark, while his brother was somewhat stouter of build, with fair, curly hair. As they strolled down the street they received and returned many greetings, for both boys were well-known and popular in Bayport.

Before they reached the store they heard the shriek of the whistle and the clanging of the bell that indicated that the express was resuming its southward journey.

"Our friend can travel in peace," remarked Frank. "He got his five changed anyway."

"And the other fellow got his dollar. Everybody's happy."

They reached the store and paused outside the entrance to examine an assortment of baseball bats, discussing the relative merits and weights of each, then poked around in a tray of mitts, trying them on and agreeing that none equaled the worn and battered mitts they had at home. Finally they entered the shop, where they were greeted by the proprietor, a chubby and genial man named Moss. Mr. Moss was sitting on the counter reading a newspaper, for business was dull that afternoon, but he cast the sheet aside when they came in.

"Looking for clues?" he asked humorously, as they came in.

As sons of Fenton Hardy, and as amateur detectives of some ability in their own right, the boys were frequently the butt of jesting remarks concerning their hobby, but they invariably took them in the spirit of good-natured raillery in which they were meant.

"No clues here," continued Mr. Moss. "You won't find a single, solitary clue in the place. I had a crate of awfully nice bank robbery clues in yesterday, but they've all been snapped up. I expect some nice murder clues in to-morrow morning, if you'd care to wait that long. Or perhaps you'd like me to order you a few kidnapping clues. Size eight and a half, guaranteed not to wear, tear or tarnish."

Mr. Moss rattled on, with an air of great gravity, burst into a roar of laughter at his own joke, then swung his feet against the side of the counter.

"Well, boys, what'll it be?" he asked, rubbing his eyes, as the two brothers grinned at him. "What can I do for you?"

"We want some pie-plates," said Joe. "Three."

"Small ones, I suppose," said Mr. Moss,

then chuckled hugely as the boys looked at him
in indignation.

"I should say not," returned Frank.  "The
biggest you've got."

Mr. Moss laughed very much at this also,
and swung himself down from the counter and
went in search of the pie-plates.  He returned
eventually with three that seemed to be of the
required size and quality.

"Wrap 'em up," said Frank, throwing the
five dollar bill on the counter.

Mr. Moss wrapped up the plates, then
picked up the bill and went over to the cash
register.  He rang up the amount of the sale
and was about to put the money in the till when
he suddenly hesitated, then held the bill up to
the light.  Slowly, he came back to the counter,
rubbing the bill between thumb and forefinger,
feeling its texture and minutely examining the
surface.

"Where did you get this bill, boys?" he
asked seriously.

"We just changed it for a stranger on the
train," answered Frank.  "What's the matter
with it?"

"Looks bad to me," replied Mr. Moss dubi-
ously.  "I'm afraid I can't take a chance on
it."

He handed the bill back to Frank, then indicated the package on the counter.

"What are you going to do about the plates?" he asked. "Have you any other money besides that bill?"

"Not a nickel," said Joe. "At least, not enough to pay for the plates. But do you really think the bill is no good?"

"I've handled a lot of them. It doesn't look good to me. I tell you what you'd better do. Take it over to the bank across the street and ask the cashier what he thinks of it."

The boys looked at one another in dismay. It had never occurred to them that there might be anything wrong with the money. Now it dawned on them that there had been something suspicious about the affable stranger's request. Had they really been victimized?

"We'll do that," agreed Frank. "Come on, Joe. Keep those plates for us, Mr. Moss. If the bill is bad we'll be back with some real money later on."

They crossed the street to the bank and went up to the cashier's cage. They knew the cashier well and he smiled at them as Frank pushed the five dollar bill under the grating.

"Want it changed?" he asked.

"We want to know if it's good, first."

The cashier, a sharp-featured, elderly man with spectacles, then took a sharp glance at the bill. He pursed up his lips as he felt the texture of the paper. Then he flicked the bill across to them again.

"Sorry," he said. "You've been stung, boys. It's counterfeit."

"Counterfeit!" exclaimed Frank.

"You aren't the first one who has been fooled. There's been a lot of counterfeit money going around the past few days. It's very cleverly done and it's apt to fool any one who isn't used to handling a lot of bills. Where did you get it?"

"A fellow got off the train and asked us to change it for him."

The cashier nodded.

"And by now he is miles away, probably getting ready to work the same trick at the next station. I guess you'll have to pocket your loss, boys. It's tough luck."

# CHAPTER II

## COUNTERFEIT MONEY

THE Hardy boys left the bank, feeling at once foolish and wrathful.

"Stung!" declared Frank. "Stung by a counterfeit bill! Oh, if the fellows hear of this we'll never hear the end of it!"

"What a fine pair of greenhorns we must have looked to that slick stranger! I'd like to lay my hands on him for about five seconds. I'll bet he's been laughing to himself ever since about how easily we were fooled."

"I'll say we were easy. We hadn't a suspicion in the world."

"After all," Joe remarked, "that bill might have fooled any one. You can't deny that it looks mighty like a real five."

They halted on the corner and again examined the money. Only an experienced eye could have detected any difference between the counterfeit bill and a genuine one. It was crisp and new and appeared in every respect identical with any bona fide five dollar bill that had ever been legitimately issued by the Federal Government.

"If we were dishonest we could palm this off on almost any one, just as we had it palmed off on us," said Joe. "Oh, well—live and learn. I hate to think of that fellow laughing at us, though. It's a nice price to pay for a lesson not to be too trustful of strangers after this."

"It cost me more than it cost you," Frank pointed out. "It was just my luck that I had three dollars on me and you had only two."

This phase of the matter had not occurred to Joe before, so he felt considerably more cheerful in the thought that he had not, after all, been the chief loser.

They went back to the store and dolefully reported to Mr. Moss that he had been right in his surmise about the bill.

"It was bad, all right," Frank told him. "The cashier took one look at it, and that was enough."

Mr. Moss nodded sympathetically.

"Well, it's too bad you were stung," he said. "But I'd rather it was you than me. In business, we have to be careful. As a matter of fact, I think it would have fooled me, only the bank warned me this morning that there was some counterfeit money going around and that I'd better be on my guard against any new

bills. The minute I saw your five was fresh
and new I got suspicious. It's certainly a
clever imitation. Whoever is putting the stuff
out is a real artist at that game."

"We'll be back for the pie-plates later,"
promised Joe. "But we didn't want you to
think we were trying to pass bad money on
you."

Mr. Moss laughed at the idea.

"The Hardy boys pass counterfeit money!"
he exclaimed. "I know you better than that, I
hope. I'll keep the plates for you, or you
can take them now and bring back the money
later. *Good* money, though," he added, wag-
ging his finger at them.

"We'll be back," they told him.

They went toward the station to wait for
the local train on which they expected their
father to arrive, and while they waited, sitting
on a platform bench, they gloomily discussed
the imposition of which they had been the
victims.

"It isn't so much losing my three dollars,"
declared Frank. "It's the thought of being
fooled by such a simple trick. We should have
known that the fellow had plenty of time to get
his money changed at the lunch counter or at
the cigar stand, or even the ticket office. Instead of that we dug into our pockets like
lambs—"

"Lambs don't have pockets," Joe pointed out.

"All the better for them. They're so innocent they'd be fleeced of everything they put in 'em, anyway. Just like us. We handed over all our money to a total stranger and let him give us a bad bill that we didn't even take the trouble to look at. I wish somebody would kick me all around the block."

While the Hardy boys are sitting on the bench, gloomily awaiting the arrival of their father and preparing to tell him of how they had been fooled by the stranger, it will not be out of place to introduce them still further to the readers of this volume.

As related in the first volume of this series, "The Hardy Boys: The Tower Treasure," Frank and Joe Hardy were the sons of Fenton Hardy, a private detective of international fame. Mr. Hardy, who had been for many years on the New York police force and who had later resigned to carry on a private detective practice, was a criminologist of note. He knew by sight and by reputation most of the notorious criminals of his day, and his mastery over all the branches of his profession was such as to place him at the very forefront of American detectives. So great had been the demand for his services in solving the mysteries of crimes that had baffled the detective forces of other cities that he had found it much more lucrative to carry on a practice of his own than to remain attached to the service in any one city, even such a city as the great American metropolis.

Fenton Hardy, with his wife, Laura Hardy, and their two sons, Frank and Joe, had accordingly moved to Bayport, a city of about fifty thousand inhabitants, situated on Barmet Bay, on the Atlantic Ocean. There Frank and Joe had gone to school until now they were in the Bayport high school. Both boys were fully conscious of the fame of their father and were eager to follow in his footsteps, although their mother had expressed a desire that they fit themselves for some less hazardous and more conventional profession.

However, the Hardy boys had inherited much of their father's ability and deductive talent. Already they had aided in solving two mysteries that had kept Bayport by the ears. As related in "The Hardy Boys: The Tower Treasure," they had solved the mystery of the theft of valuable jewels and bonds from Tower Mansion, after even Fenton Hardy himself had been unable to discover where the thief had hidden the loot. In the second volume of the series, "The Hardy Boys: The House on the Cliff," has been told how the Hardy boys discovered the haunt of a gang of smugglers who were operating in Barmet Bay. In this case they had received a substantial reward, as Federal agents had tried in vain to locate the smugglers' base of activities for many months.

Following the adventures at the house on the cliff an uneventful winter and spring had passed, the brothers devoting themselves to their studies and to an occasional winter holiday. Christmas had come with many presents, and now warm weather was once more at hand.

Because of the pride they took in their achievements as amateur detectives, the Hardy boys felt very keenly the ignominy of being so easily fooled by the stranger who had passed the counterfeit money upon them.

"Dad will have the laugh on us now," muttered Joe, as they heard the distant whistle of the approaching train.

"Well, we'll tell him about it, anyway. Who knows but what a big case might arise out of this?"

The afternoon local pulled into the station, and Fenton Hardy stepped down from the parlor car, bag in hand, light coat over one arm. He was a tall, dark-haired man of about forty years of age. He had a quick, pleasant smile for his sons and he shook hands with them warmly.

"How's mother?" he asked, after the first greetings.

"She's fine," replied Frank. "She said there'd be something special for supper to-night, seeing you're back."

"Good! And what have you two been do-ing? Kept out of mischief, I hope."

"Well, we've kept out of mischief," said Joe; "but we haven't kept out of trouble."

"What's the matter?"

"We just got fooled by a smart stranger who stepped off the express. It cost us five dollars."

"How did that happen?"

"He asked us to change a five dollar bill for him—"

"Ah, ha!" exclaimed Fenton Hardy, raising his eyebrows. "And what then?"

"It was counterfeit."

Mr. Hardy looked grave.

"Have you got it with you?"

"Yes," answered Frank, producing the bill. "I don't think we can be blamed such an awful lot for being fooled. It certainly looks mighty like a good one."

Fenton Hardy put down his bag and ex-amined the bill closely for a moment. Then he folded it up and put it in his waistcoat pocket.

"I'll take care of this, if you don't mind," he said, picking up his bag and beginning to walk toward the station exit. "As it happens, I know something about this money."

"What do you mean, dad?" asked Frank quickly.

"I don't mean that I know anything about this particular five dollar bill, but I know something about this counterfeit money in general. As a matter of fact, that is why this trip took me longer than I had thought it would. When I finished the case that originally took me away, the Government called me in on this counterfeit money case."

"Is there a lot of it going around?"

"Too much. Within the past few weeks the East has been flooded with it, and the circulation seems to be spreading. There seems to be a central counterfeiting plant somewhere, with experts in charge of it, and they are turning out imitation bills so clever that the average person can hardly detect them. The Federal authorities are worrying a great deal about it."

"And this is one of the bills?"

"It looks just like some of the others that have been turned in, although chiefly they have been dealing in tens and twenties. The man who stepped off the train was probably one of their agents, trying to convert as much of the counterfeit money into good cash as he could. When he saw that you were only boys he thought there would be a better chance of getting change for five dollars than ten. Then, of course, he may only have been some one who had been fooled by the counterfeit and decided to get rid of it by passing it on to some one else.''

''I wish he had asked us to change one of his counterfeit tens, instead,'' mourned Joe. ''We would have been five dollars to the good.''

## CHAPTER III

### THE HARDY BOYS AT SCHOOL

IF the boys had any lingering hopes that their school chums would not hear of the manner in which they had been fooled, these hopes were quickly removed next morning.

Scarcely had Frank and Joe ascended the concrete steps of Bayport High than Chet Morton, a stout chubby boy of about sixteen, one of their closest friends, a lad with a passion for practical jokes, came solemnly toward them with a green tobacco coupon in his hand.

"Just the fellows I'm looking for," he chirped. "My great-grandmother just died in Abyssinia and I'm trying to raise the railway fare to go to the funeral. How about changing this hundred?"

There was a roar of laughter from about a dozen boys who were standing about, for Chet had evidently acquainted them all with the affair of the previous day. How he had learned of it, Frank and Joe could not imagine.

18

They grinned good-naturedly, although Joe blushed furiously.

"What's the matter?" asked Chet innocently. "Can't you change it? You don't mean to tell me you can't change my hundred dollar bill? Please, kind young gentlemen, please change my hundred dollar bill, for if you don't I'm sure nobody else will and then I won't be able to go to my great-grandmother's funeral in Abyssinia." He wiped away an imaginary tear.

"Sorry," said Frank gravely. "We're not in the money-changing business."

"You mean you're not in it any more," pointed out Chet. "You were in the business yesterday, I know. What's the matter—retire on your profits?"

"Yes, we quit."

"I don't blame you." Suddenly Chet struck an attitude of exaggerated surprise. "Why, bless my soul, I do believe this bill is bad!" He peered at the flimsy tobacco coupon very closely, then whipped a small magnifying glass from his pocket and squinted through it. At last he raised his head, with a sigh. "Yes, sir, it's bad. It's counterfeit. One of the cleverest counterfeits I ever saw. If it hadn't been for the fact that there is no hundred dollar mark on it and if it hadn't been that there is a picture of the president of the El

Ropo Tobacco Company instead of George Washington, I'd have been completely fooled. Isn't it lucky that you boys didn't change it for me? Isn't it lucky? Congratulations, young sirs. Congratulations!"

He shook Frank and Joe warmly by the hand, in the meantime keeping a very solemn face, while the other lads surged about in a laughing group and joined in the "kidding."

They jested unmercifully about the incident of the counterfeit five dollars, but the Hardy boys took it all in good part. The news had leaked out through Mr. Moss, who had told Jerry Gilroy, one of the Hardy boys' chums, about the affair just a short while after they had left the store the previous afternoon. Jerry had lost no time acquainting Chet and the others with the details.

"If you keep on changing money for strangers you won't have much left out of those rewards," declared Phil Cohen, a diminutive, black-haired Jewish boy who was one of their friends. He was referring to the money the Hardy boys had received in rewards for their work in the Tower Mansion case and for helping run down the smugglers.

"Oh, I guess we still have a few dollars," replied Frank smilingly. "We have enough in the bank to buy a motorboat with, anyway."

"What's that?" asked Chet quickly. "Are you getting a motorboat?"

The Hardy boys nodded. Their chums were immediately interested.

"Put me down for one of the first passengers," shouted "Biff" Hooper, a tall, broad-shouldered boy who had just pushed his way through the circle.

"We're thinking of getting one like Tony Prito's," said Joe.

"I wish is was mine!" exclaimed Tony. His father, one of the most respected citizens in the Italian colony of Bayport, owned a speedy motorboat which had proved of great service to the Hardy boys in their conflict with the smugglers of Barmet Bay. "But if you're getting a boat at all you can't do any better than get one just like it."

"Dad told us last night we could get one as long as we stayed in the bay and along the coast with it. He was afraid we might get ambitious and try crossing the Atlantic."

"Well," remarked Jerry Gilroy, "I see where our summer baseball league is shot to pieces now."

"Why?"

"You'll be out in that boat every minute of your spare time. It was bad enough when you had the motorcycles. You were both always roaming around the country on them, but now we'll never be able to find you at all.   There goes the best pitcher and shortstop of my team together."

Jerry looked very glum as he said this, for he was an ardent ball fan and he had been much in the forefront in organizing a league for the summer months.  Frank Hardy was one of the best pitchers in the school, and Joe could cover short in a manner that was the envy of his companions, but in spite of their natural ability for the game, the Hardy boys had always shown a preference for outings instead of baseball.

"I'd rather go out for a whole day on a motorcycle or in a motorboat than play a dozen ball games," said Frank.

This was rank heresy to Jerry, who could not bear any reflections on his beloved game.

"Gosh, I don't know what's to become of you two!  Can't I count on you for any games at all?"

"Sure you can," promised Frank.  "We're not going to *live* in the motorboat."

"If you go fooling around Barmet Reefs on a stormy day in the old tub you'll *die* in it, though," snickered Chet.

"That'll be about enough from you," warned Frank, giving him a friendly dig in the ribs. Then, turning to Jerry, he went on: "We'll play on your team, but we won't spend all our time outside of meal-hours in practising."

"Well, I suppose I should be satisfied. We can't have everything. But I'd imagine you'd *like* to practise."

"They don't need to," declared Chet. "That's why you have to spend all your spare time learning how to catch. Even now you're not much good at it." He winked at Tony Prito, who was standing behind Jerry. "Why, I'll bet you can't catch a measly little fly—like this—look—"

He took a baseball out of his pocket and threw it lightly into the air. It did not go very high and it was a ridiculously easy catch for any one. As for Jerry Gilroy, who was really a star outfielder, it was scarcely worth the effort. He had but to step back a pace and the ball was his.

"Can't I?" he said, somewhat nettled by Chet's words. The ball arched through the air and descended directly toward him. He stepped back, prepared to make the easy catch.

But Tony Prito had caught Chet's wink and knew what it meant, for they had carefully rehearsed the trick between them. As soon as Chet had thrown the ball, Tony knelt on his hands and knees on the grass immediately behind Jerry. For all his seeming carelessness, Chet had thrown the ball just far enough so that Jerry would have to step back to make the catch.

Jerry collided with the recumbent figure behind him, he staggered, lost his balance and tumbled over Tony Prito, while the baseball thumped into the grass. The other boys, who had seen the joke from the start, laughed uproariously as Jerry picked himself up and betook himself in pursuit of the already fleeing Tony, while Chet, with an air of vast satisfaction, picked up the baseball.

"I knew he couldn't catch it," he said, with all the airy disdain of a minor prophet.

Just then the gong in the main hall of Bayport High began to clang, summoning the students to their classes, and the boys crowded through the wide doorway.

# CHAPTER IV

## ANOTHER VICTIM

WHEN he took his place in class that morning, Frank Hardy glanced over at the desk, two aisles away, where Callie Shaw was sitting.

Callie, a brown-haired, brown-eyed miss with a quick, vivacious manner, was one of the prettiest girls attending Bayport high school. She was Frank's favorite of all the girls in the city, and each morning he glanced over at her desk and never failed to receive a bright and fleeting smile that somehow made the dusty classroom seem a trifle less drab and monotonous, and when she was not there it always seemed that the day had gotten away to a bad start.

She was there this morning, but she was gazing soberly at her books and she failed to return Frank's glance with her usual smile. This was something so utterly extraordinary that Frank gazed at her, open-mouthed, for a second or so until, recollecting himself, he turned to his own books and proceeded to spend much of the time until recess in a state of helpless wonderment. Like the average boy under such circumstances, he racked his brains trying to recollect what he could have done that might have offended Callie. But there seemed to be no solution to the mystery.

Perhaps she had heard of how he had been fooled by the stranger yesterday. Perhaps she felt contempt for him because he had been so easily outwitted. This was one of his wild surmises, but he rejected it because it was not like Callie to be angry about anything unless there was good reason for her displeasure. At last he gave it up and tried to dismiss the matter from his mind, but several times during the morning he cast covert glances in her direction.

But Callie was plainly worried and downcast. She seldom raised her eyes from her books, she answered the teacher's questions in a most abstracted manner, and altogether it appeared that there was something on her mind beyond schoolwork.

When recess came she walked slowly out of the room, not mingling with the other girls. Frank saw her go outside toward the campus, where she sat down on the grass by herself, watching an impromptu basketball game and declining all requests to join in the fun.

He went over to her and flung himself down on the grass beside the girl.

"What's the matter, Callie?"

She looked up at him and smiled faintly.

"Hello, Frank, where did you drop from?"

"I've been sitting right across from you in school all morning and this is the first time you've noticed that I'm alive."

"I'm sorry, Frank. I didn't mean to be rude. I've got something on my mind this morning, that's all."

"Trouble?"

She nodded.

"What about?"

"Money."

He was puzzled by this remark. Callie lived with her cousin, Miss Pollie Shaw, the proprietor of a beauty parlor in the city, and although Miss Shaw was not rich, she made a comfortable living. Therefore, when Frank heard Callie say that she was worried about money he was naturally puzzled. Callie's parents lived in the country, but they sent their daughter frequent remittances to pay the expenses of her education in Bayport.

"What's the matter?" he asked. "Didn't your allowance come?"

"No, it isn't that. I'm all right. It's Pollie. She lost some money. More than she could afford."

"Lost some? How was that?"

"She lost fifty dollars last night."

Frank whistled.

"Whew! That's a lot of money."

"It certainly is. The worst of it is that Pollie had just made the final payment on some new electrical fixtures in the shop and it had left her pretty short of cash. I feel bad about it for her sake."

"How did it happen?"

"A woman came into the store last night and bought some beauty preparations, quite a large order. It amounted to about twelve dollars and she had nothing less than a fifty dollar bill in her purse. Pollie had that much money in the till, for it was near the end of the day, and she didn't like to lose the order, so she changed the bill."

Frank nodded soberly. He knew now what had happened.

"And the money was counterfeit," he said.

"Why, how did you know?" exclaimed Callie.

"I was fooled yesterday myself." Frank then went on to tell Callie how he and Joe had been victimized by the stranger on the station platform. "Dad says there is a lot of this counterfeit money being circulated," he said. "They certainly aren't losing much time in getting rid of it around Bayport. Gee, first a five and now a fifty! I'm sure sorry that Pollie is out that much money."

"Yes, it's a big amount," declared Callie.

"Of course, she'll get along, but no one likes to lose that much."

"Did she know the woman?"

"Oh, no. She was a total stranger. She was rather handsome and was well dressed. Pollie didn't suspect anything wrong. As a matter of fact, it wasn't until she picked up the paper after work last night and read that the banks had issued a warning about counterfeit money that she began to think about it. So she called up Mr. Wilkins, who works in one of the banks, and he came over and took a look at the bill. He said right away that it was no good, although he admitted it was so cleverly done that any one might be fooled by it."

"Just what they said about my five. Did Pollie tell the police?"

"I suppose she has told them by now. But she gave me the bill and asked me to turn it over to your father."

"Good! Dad happens to be working along those lines just now. Have you got the bill with you now?"

"It's in my purse in the cloakroom. I'll let you have it at lunch hour."

So when school was dismissed at noon Callie gave Frank the counterfeit fifty dollar bill. Frank examined it closely. Like the five dollar bill he and Joe had changed for the plausible stranger the previous day, it was crisp and

new. Frank had seen very few fifty dollar
bills in his life, either genuine or otherwise, but
he realized that this specimen was a very good
imitation. The mere fact that such bills are
not often seen by the average person no doubt
rendered it easier to pass without being readily
detected.

"I'll show this to my father," he promised
Callie. "I'm afraid it won't do much good.
Pollie will have to stand her loss, unless she
can trace the woman who passed the bad bill
on her, but perhaps this will help dad find the
source of all this counterfeit money."

"Goodness knows how many poor people are
being victimized just as Pollie was," said the
girl. "I hope they catch the people who are
at the bottom of it."

When Joe joined Frank on the school steps
Frank told him about the incident at the beauty
parlor and of how Pollie Shaw had lost fifty
dollars in goods and money to the strange
woman.

"Of course," said Frank, "she may have
been perfectly innocent in passing that fifty
dollar bill, and perhaps she didn't realize it
was counterfeit, but I'm beginning to think this
gang has a number of people traveling around
getting rid of the imitation bills."

"Once they get them into circulation they'll
go from hand to hand until the banks check

them up. Somebody is bound to lose in the end, and usually it's the honest person who finds out that the money is bad and won't pass it any further. The crooked ones will just try to get rid of it as quickly as they can.''

When they reached home Frank told his father about Pollie Shaw and handed over the counterfeit bill.

"So they're dealing in fifties now!" exclaimed Fenton Hardy, as he looked at the money.

"Do you think it's made by the people who turned out that bad five that we got stung on?" Joe asked.

Mr. Hardy drew a magnifying glass from his vest pocket and make a close scrutiny of the bill. "It seems to have been printed on the same press but I'm not sure," he announced at last. "These things are so cleverly done that it would take an expert to notice any differences." He proceeded then to examine the five dollar bill, comparing it closely with the fifty, and at last he put the glass back into his pocket.

"I'm practically certain that these bills were issued from the same press. The paper seems to be of the same kind, just a shade lighter than the paper used in genuine money, and there are certain little differences in the engraving that are almost identical on each bill. Miss

Shaw won't mind if I keep this, will she?" he asked Frank.

"She asked me to give it to you."

"I'll send both these bills to an expert in the city and we'll get his opinion on it."

Mrs. Hardy, a pretty, fair-haired woman, sighed.

"I'm sure I don't know what the world's coming to," she said, "when men will make bad money and know that poor people are going to lose by it. It's a shame."

"There's nothing some of them won't stop at when it comes to filling their own pockets," declared her husband. "But perhaps when the expert sends me his report on these bills I'll have something more to work on. If it turns out that there is one central gang circulating this money we'll all have to be on the lookout."

# CHAPTER V

## CURING THE JOKER

HARD work in school occupied the attention of the boys for the rest of the week, for examination time was near, and even Jerry Gilroy was obliged to dismiss baseball from his mind in a frantic attempt to catch up with his geometry and Latin, that somehow appeared to keep perpetually ahead of him. Frank and Joe sweated over the ablative absolute and grumbled over the heroic exploits that could be resurrected from the deathless lines of Cæsar and Virgil if one could but distinguish verbs from nouns, and wondered, as schoolboys have wondered from time immemorial, why they should be obliged to concern themselves with things that happened two thousand years ago and more when they might better be outside playing.

When Friday night came they emerged from the haze of declensions and vocabularies, axioms and theorems, equations and symbols in which they had been engulfed all week and

decided that Saturday should see them as far
away from school as possible.

"Let's get out of the city altogether," suggested Frank, as the Hardy boys left the classroom on Friday afternoon. "What say we all
go for a hike out into the country?"

"Suits me," agreed Chet. "No motorcycles
either. Let's walk."

"Good idea," Jerry Gilroy approved. "Unless," he said hopefully, "you fellows would
rather come up to the campus and have baseball practice."

"Another smart remark like that out of you
and I'll practise my famous left hook on your
jaw," warned Biff Hooper, squaring off in a
pugilistic attitude. "We don't want to see or
hear of this school again until Monday morning, and that'll be too soon."

"All right, all right," said Jerry placatingly.
"I just thought I'd mention it."

"And I just think you'll forget about
it," said Chet. "You'll come along on this
hike with us. Here, have an apple and keep
quiet."

He dug into the inexhaustible recesses of his
pockets and produced a slightly shopworn
apple, which he thrust into Jerry's hands.
"There, see if that'll keep you quiet for a
while."

Jerry, who could never resist anything in

the nature of food, accepted the donation eagerly.

"Where shall we go on this hike?" he asked, raising the fruit to his lips.

"I was thinking we could go up to Carl Stummer's farm," suggested Joe. "Mother was saying she wondered if Stummer would let her have any cherries to can this year. This would be a good time to ask him."

"Suits me," said Jerry, taking a prodigious bite of the apple.

Then an expression of pained surprise crossed his face to be replaced by a look of ghastly realization. Tears spurted to his eyes and his jaws worked convulsively. Then he emitted a gurgle of agony, spluttered, spat out the apple and began to dance around on the pavement, waving his arms in the air.

"Indian war dance!" commented Chet gravely, clapping his hands. "Fine work, Jerry. Do it again."

"Pepper!" spluttered Jerry. "I'm burning up! Water!"

"Call the fire brigade," advised Chet, bursting into a shriek of laughter.

The other lads gazed at their companion in amazement until his wild antics became too much for them and they all roared as Jerry continued his frantic splutterings. Wildly, the victim turned toward the school again. There was a water fountain near the front door and he headed toward it, but his eyes were so full of tears from the mouthful of red pepper that he had gulped when he bit into the hollow apple that he did not see a flower-bed in his path.

Jerry stumbled over the wire border and sprawled full length among the flowers.

The janitor, a cantankerous individual named MacBane, had been standing near by watching the performance with a broad grin on his usually dour features. But when he saw Jerry fall into his precious flower-bed he gave a roar of fury.

"Awa' wi' ye!" he bellowed. "Awa' frae ma flowers, ye young limb! I'll hae ye reported!"

MacBane always lapsed into broad Scotch when his temper was aroused. The rest of the boys scattered, fearing the wrath to come. Jerry managed to scramble out of the flower-bed just as the janitor reached him. He jumped out of reach of the outstretched hand, with the result that MacBane lost his balance and overstepped the border, treading on some choice blossoms and getting tangled up in the wire.

Jerry made for the fountain and was already taking deep gulps of the cool water when Mac-Bane, now spluttering unintelligible phrases that could only have been understood in the remotest reaches of Caledonia, got out of the flower-bed and thundered toward him. With a longing glance at the spouting water, for his raging thirst was not yet appeased, and with a fearful glance at the approaching janitor, Jerry turned and fled.

He joined his laughing companions at the street corner, and with a shame-faced air admitted that the joke had been on him. MacBane gave up the chase, vowing threats of vengeance on the following Monday.

"He'll forget all about it by then," assured Phil.

"I won't forget about it," declared Jerry. "Next time anybody offers me an apple I'll ask for an orange instead. You can't very well fill *that* with pepper. I'll get even with you, Chet."

"You're welcome to try," replied the practical joker cheerfully. "But in the meantime let's plan this trip for to-morrow."

As a result of their arrangements, the Hardy boys and their chums met in the barn back of the Hardy home early the next morning, all outfitted for a hike into the country. Each lad carried a substantial lunch, their mothers realizing that the noonday meal by the roadside is one of the chief features of such an outing. Phil and Tony were late, and the other boys put in the time by exercising in the Hardy

boys' well equipped gymnasium, to which purpose the barn had been converted. Biff Hooper
practised left hooks and uppercuts with desperate intensity and battered the punching bag
until it hummed; Chet almost broke his neck
attempting some complicated maneuvers on
the parallel bars that were meant as an imitation of a circus bareback rider; Jerry contem-
plated his lunch and wondered if it were too
soon after breakfast for a piece of pie.

Phil Cohen and Tony Prito arrived together
and the boys started off at last, trudging along
the broad highway in the early morning sunlight, whistling away in the best of spirits.
They were decorous enough while they were
in the city limits, but once they struck the dusty
country roads their natural activity asserted
itself and they wrestled and tripped one
another, ran impromptu races, picked berries
by the roadside and laughed and shouted without a care in the world.

The road skirted the Willow River, which
ran among the farms and hills back of Bayport,
through a pleasant, pastoral country. Toward
the middle of the morning the boys left the
road and struck out beneath the trees toward
a secluded spot on the river, where they en-
joyed a swim. For over an hour they splashed
about in the cool water. Chet was the first to
come ashore, and the others would have re-

mained much longer had it not been for the discovery that their thoughtful companion, after getting dressed, was busying himself in the time-honored pastime of tying their clothes into knots.

Whereupon they scrambled out of the water and chased the chubby one into the shelter of some bushes, whence they were unable to pursue him further because the thorns hurt their bare feet and they were forced to retreat, hopping, toward the river bank while Chet jeered at them from the covert.

"Chaw on the beef!" he cried, in the time-honored way.

"Just you wait!" spluttered Joe, chewing on a knot with all his might.

"Am waiting," was the cheerful retort of the joker.

"We'll skin you alive!" muttered Jerry.

"And salt you," added Frank.

But when they had untied the knots they gave chase and the plump jester was soon winded, although he had a good start. He puffed and panted as they chased him down the road in the dust. They caught up to him at the entrance to the lane leading into Carl Stummer's farm, forcibly divested him of his hiking-boots, socks and necktie and proceeded to wreak revenge.

"We'll cure you of practical jokes for a

while," promised Frank, with a grin, as he cast one boot into a field wherein a bad-natured bull was grazing, and the other into a field at the other side of the lane, with a heavy growth of thistles around the fence.

"See if you're as good at untying knots as you are at tying them," added Jerry, as he twisted Chet's necktie into a veritable Chinese puzzle.

"And now see how it feels to walk around in your bare feet," suggested Phil, as he hung one of Chet's socks over the limb of a tree some distance down the road and placed the other in the middle of a clump of brambles.

Biff Hooper and Tony then released the protesting Chet. They had been sitting on him in the middle of the lane while the others were performing their kindly offices. "We'll see you down at the farm," said Biff airily, as the lads went chuckling down the lane in the direction of Stummer's place.

Spluttering and vowing threats, Chet was forced to retrieve his clothes. When he sought to regain his boot from the pasture the bull saw him and rushed toward him with a bellow. Chet, in bare feet, just reached the fence in time and tumbled over into the bushes with the rescued boot. Then he had to step gingerly through the thistle patch in the other field before he could get the other boot. After that he had to climb a tree before he could reach one sock, and go plunging through the brambles before he could regain the other. When the laughing boys last saw him he was sitting by the roadside picking thistles from his feet and gazing hopelessly at his necktie.

"He's cured for a while now," chuckled Joe, as the boys came up into the barnyard of Stummer's farm.

"Cure him? Never!" exclaimed Frank. "He'll be making us all step before the day is out."

# CHAPTER VI

## THE OLD MILL

CARL STUMMER, a lanky, shambling old farmer with drooping shoulders, a drooping mustache and a drooping pipe, was just coming in from the fields when the boys came through the barnyard gate.

How he managed to chew a straw and smoke a pipe perpetually at the same time was always a fascinating mystery, but he could do it and always seemed to derive a great deal of satisfaction from the feat, stopping only to change the straw or fill the pipe at intervals. Some people had been known to have seen him without the straw and some had seen him without the pipe, but no one had ever seen him without one or the other.

Chet Morton always stated it as a grave fact that Carl Stummer slept with his pipe in his mouth and a supply of fresh straws constantly by his bedside and that he changed them in his sleep.

" 'Lo, boys!" he called, taking a firmer

grip of the pipestem. "And what brings you here?"

"How's the cherry crop, Mr. Stummer?" asked Frank.

"Fair to middlin'," replied Mr. Stummer doubtfully.

This was a good sign, as Carl Stummer was rarely known to express an encouraging opinion about anything. If he said crops were poor, one might be reasonably certain that they were really fair. If he said they were "fair to middlin'" it might be inferred that they were excellent.

"Mother wants to know if you can let her have cherries to can this year."

Mr. Stummer chewed with relish at the straw.

"Most probably she kin," he agreed.

"She wanted to speak for them so that you'd keep her in mind at cherry-picking time."

"I'll remember," promised Stummer. "Mrs. Hardy has always been a good customer of mine. You tell her she can have all of them cherries that she wants."

"Thanks, Mr. Stummer. That's all we called about."

The farmer looked at them. His hands were plunged deep in the pockets of his faded overalls. The straw waggled beneath the drooping mustache.

"Out for a hike?" he ventured.

"Yes. We thought it would be a good day for it."

"Yeah, pretty fair day for hikin'," agreed Mr. Stummer, glancing at the sky to make sure. "Where you thinkin' of goin'?"

"Oh, we don't know. Just around the country."

"Yeah? Not goin' down by the old mill, are you?"

"Turner's old mill?" asked Joe. "Down by the deserted road?"

"That's the place. Down by the river."

"Well, we hadn't thought particularly about going down there. Why do you ask?"

The straw waggled more violently than ever. Mr. Stummer took a long drag at the pipe, which was in imminent danger of going out.

"Oh, I dunno," he said, with a reflective sigh. "Just thought I'd say somethin' about it. I wouldn't go down there if I was you."

"Why not?" inquired Frank. "I know the place is deserted and it's almost falling down, but we can keep out of danger, can't we?"

"It ain't deserted now."

"What do you mean?"

"There's three fellows running the mill now. Funny fellows they are. Been there for a couple of weeks."

The boys looked at one another in surprise. Turner's flour mill was located on a wild part of the Willow River. It had once been on a main road, but the construction of a new highway had left it on a deserted loop which was now seldom traversed. The mill had been abandoned for several years and seemed to have outlived its usefulness. No one had ever expected that the mill wheel would turn again.

"Are they running it as a flour mill?" asked Frank.

Stummer nodded.

"They don't do much outside grindin'. I sent 'em some of my wheat, but their prices was too high. They nearly skinned me alive, so they don't need to expect any more trade from me. I'll send my grain into Bayport after this, where I've always been sendin' it."

"How do they expect to make a living then?"

"They ain't lookin' for trade from the farmers. Matter of fact, I don't think they want it. They told me they're gettin' up some new kind of breakfast foods that the doctors are all goin' to take up. There's somethin' secret about it," went on Stummer, warming to the mystery. "They ain't sayin' anything until they get their patents. Why, they won't even let a man go through the mill."

"Three men, you say?"

"Yeah. Three fellers. Sort of onpleasant lookin' chaps. And there's a boy there too. I

forgot about him. Looks somethin' like you,"
he said, pointing to Joe.

"Have you ever seen any of them before?"
Stummer shook his head.

"I guess they come from the city," he
hazarded. "They come away down here so
they could be quiet and work at this here breakfast food stuff of theirs without bein' bothered.
That's why I said you shouldn't go down
there. They don't like people hangin' around."

"Makes me curious to see the place," put in
Jerry.

The other boys gave murmurs of agreement.

"Go along if you like," said Stummer,
shrugging his shoulders. "It ain't none of my
affair. Just thought I'd tell you, that's all.
They don't like strangers around."

"We won't bother them," promised Frank.
"What do you say, fellows? Should we take
a trip around that way or should we not?"

As usual, the mere fact that something of a
mystery surrounded the old mill made all the
boys eager to turn their steps in that direction.

"We'll go down the old road, anyway," said
Joe. "I'd like to get a look at the place. It'll
give us somewhere to go."

"Sure," agreed Phil. "We can eat our
lunch on the way."

"The vote seems to be in favor of it," said
Frank, with a smile.

"Well," drawled Stummer, chewing vigorously at the straw, "don't blame me if you get chased away from the mill. I've warned you."

His eyes twinkled. His whole purpose in telling the lads of the mystery that surrounded the mill had been to send them in that direction, for he realized the attraction the place would have for the boys when they knew that the mill was running again. He was rather curious, too, about the three men who were in charge of the place and he thought that perhaps the boys might pick up some information that he had been unable to get.

"Have a good hike," he said, as he turned to go back to the farmhouse. "Don't get into any trouble."

"We won't," they assured him, and forthwith started back down the lane.

They met Chet, who had by this time managed to retrieve his belongings and was trudging along in the dust meditating ways and means of getting even with his companions. He was not vindictive and he had taken the joke in good part, grinning cheerfully as he saw them approach.

"Think you're pretty smart, don't you?" he said, in mock resentment, as they came near. "I've got so many thistles in my feet you'll have to carry me home now."

With that he began to limp in an exaggerated

manner, as though he had been completely crippled by his efforts to regain his socks and shoes.

"We wouldn't carry you to the end of the lane," said Frank promptly. "You'd better keep your feet moving if you want to come with us."

"Where are you going?"

"Down to the old mill. Stummer tells us the place is running again."

"Hurray!" shouted Chet. "I'll race you!" and, forgetting all about his tender foot-soles, he led the crowd in a mad race toward the main road.

# CHAPTER VII

## In the Mill Race

An hour later, the Hardy boys and their chums reached the vicinity of the old mill.

They had lunch in the shade of the trees along the deserted road, and it was early in the afternoon when they arrived at the top of the hill that overlooked the river.

The old mill was a sturdy structure that had once been strong and imposing but was now weatherbeaten and showed the ravages of the years. The mill wheel turned slowly, creaking painfully as though it objected to being forced to labor again after its long rest.

Outside the front door, they could see three figures, two men and a boy. At that distance it was impossible to distinguish their features, but as the lads descended the hillside and drew closer they saw that the men were middle-aged fellows, far from reassuring in appearance.

Because of Stummer's remarks, the Hardy boys and their chums took good care to keep to the shelter of the bushes as they went along the abandoned roadway, now overgrown with weeds and undergrowth. Their approach was not noticed, and at last they were standing not more than a hundred yards away from the mill, effectually concealed by the trees and shrubs.

"I don't like the looks of the men," remarked Frank, in a low voice.

"Neither do I," agreed Joe.

One of the men was apparently about fifty years of age. He had a dirty, greying beard and he wore spectacles. He was clad in a torn and stained pair of overalls and his sleeves were rolled to the elbows, revealing his blackened arms.

"For a miller, there's mighty little flour on his hands," commented Frank. "He looks more like an automobile mechanic."

The other man, who looked older, was similarly attired, but he was of a more benevolent appearance. He did not wear glasses and his shaggy brows almost hid a pair of keen, sharp eyes. He fondled his long white beard reflectively as the other man talked to him in low tones.

The boys could not overhear what the pair were saying, but they saw the boy, a fair, curly-headed youth of about fifteen, in ragged clothing, look up at the older man and say something to him.

Instantly the old fellow lost his look of benevolent reflection. He gave the boy a cuff on the ear that almost staggered him.

"Be off with you!" he ordered harshly. "Go away and play. Don't be hanging around here while we're talking."

He spoke so loudly that his words could be clearly heard by the lads hidden in the bushes. The curly-headed boy stood his ground, and evidently repeated what he had said before, for the old man at once became furious.

"Go away and play, I tell you!" he shouted in shrill tones. "I'll call you when I need you. And be sure you come in a hurry when you hear me."

He reached behind him for a heavy cane that was leaning beside the doorway and he struck out viciously at the lad with it. But the boy dodged the blow and ran off toward the mill race, while the old man watched him go, muttering imprecations.

"Leave him alone," said the other man in a guttural voice. "We've got other things to attend to than that brat."

"He's a nuisance. I'll whale the hide off him when he comes back."

"Leave him alone. Markel is waiting for us. Let's go inside."

"All right—all right," muttered the old man peevishly. He turned and followed the other through the doorway.

"Nice tempered old chap," remarked Jerry, when the pair had disappeared into the mill.

"I'll say he is," declared Joe. "I don't think either of them is up to much."

"The young fellow looks all right," Chet said. "He looks as if he has a sweet life here with those men."

Phil said:

"I thought Stummer told us there were three men running the mill."

"They said something about Markel," Frank pointed out. "He's the man who is waiting for them inside the mill. That must be the other partner."

"Let's go up and talk to the kid," suggested Joe. "Perhaps we can dig something out of him about those men. They don't seem to treat him very well, anyway."

The boy was walking along the side of the old mill race. The waters were very swift at this point, for the current was strong and the river was deep. The boy was trudging along the weatherbeaten planks, with his hands in his pockets, looking very disconsolate.

"Lonely looking boy," observed Tony. "They told him to run away and play. He looks as if he'd never played in his life."

"We'll go over and talk to him," Frank decided. "If those old chaps say anything to us about being around here we'll ask them to quote some prices on having some milling done.''

''I can do that!'' exclaimed Chet. ''Dad's a farmer, and he's often said he wished the old Turner mill was running again so he wouldn't have to haul his grain so far.''

The boys emerged from the bushes and crossed the weed-grown open space near the front of the mill. The other lad had not yet seen them. He was standing by the mill race, some distance below, gazing into the water, now and then raising his head to look at the clacking wheel that turned monotonously in showers of dripping water.

''I'm curious about this patent food story,'' Frank said. ''It's queer there wasn't anything in the papers about it. Nobody except the farmers, like Stummer, seems to have heard about the mill being taken over.''

''Oh, probably they want to keep it to themselves until everything is ready,'' Jerry pointed out. ''I'll bet you're beginning to see some kind of mystery in this already, Frank. Chances are we'll just get kicked off the premises for our pains.''

''Oh, I don't think there's any mystery about it,'' said Frank, with a smile. ''But I'm just curious to know what it's all about.''

''No law against that,'' Phil agreed. ''If this breakfast food invention of theirs turns out to be something wonderful that makes us all live about twenty years longer, we can say we were among the very first to know about it.''

By this time they had drawn closer to the mill race, and the boy standing there had raised his head and seen them.

He was a good-looking fellow, not unlike Joe Hardy in appearance, as Carl Stummer had pointed out. But his face was pinched and drawn and there was a melancholy expression in his eyes.

''Looks as if he hadn't had a square meal in a month,'' Jerry remarked.

The boy turned and began to move toward Frank and Joe.

He had gone only a few paces, however, when they saw him suddenly stumble. He had stepped upon a loose stone that had rolled from beneath his foot.

He wavered uncertainly, striving to regain his balance. Then, with a shrill cry, he toppled over into the mill race and fell with a splash into the swiftly rushing torrent of water.

''Help!'' he shouted, in terror. ''Help!''

# CHAPTER VIII

## Joe's Courage

The accident had happened so quickly that it was not for a few moments that the Hardy boys and their chums realized the lad's danger.

Then, as they saw him struggling in the torrent, they began to run toward the spot to which the lad was being rapidly carried.

Joe was in the lead, and as he ran he was taking off his coat. Just below the mill race the river was full of rocks, and the rapids dashed over them in a boiling fury of spray and foam. If the youth were ever swept into the rapids he would be doomed.

The other lads were not far behind Joe. The accident had not been seen from the mill, for no one appeared in the doorway, and the cries of the boy in the river evidently had not been heard by the men in the building.

"Help!" he was shouting. "Help!"

He was struggling in the water, being swept irresistibly on toward the deadly rapids.

"I can't swim!"

Joe reached the bank, paused to kick off his shoes, then stood poised for a moment above the rushing waters. He dived into the mill race, disappeared beneath the surface, then rose just a few yards away from the struggling boy.

The lad had already gone under once and was gasping for breath. He was just about to go under for the second time when Joe swam toward him with strong, steady strokes and grasped him by the collar.

Frantically, the boy tried to seize his rescurer, but Joe was ready for that. He knew that the unreasoning grip of a drowning person is of the utmost danger, so he managed to stay at arm's length and at the back of the boy.

"Hold steady!" he shouted, above the roar of waters. "Hold steady! Keep cool!"

His words had some effect in restoring the lad to his senses and the boy, feeling the supporting grasp on his collar, ceased his struggles.

But the danger was not yet over. The current was so strong that they were both being carried headlong downstream toward the rapids.

Joe could see the jagged rocks silhouetted against a background of flying spray and foaming water. If once they were swept into that maelstrom they would be battered to death.

He was handicapped by the weight of the boy, but he turned toward the shore and exerted all his efforts in swimming toward the bank. But he made little progress. The current was too strong for him.

The other lads, running along the bank, were watching the scene in consternation.

"He'll never make it!" declared **Jerry.** "The current is too much for him."

They could see Joe's tense face as he pitted his strength against the force of the current and desperately strove to make his way toward the bank. He was still clinging to the boy, who was commencing his struggles anew.

They were being swept closer to the rapids every moment. There were a number of rocks rising above the surface of the river just a few feet ahead, and beyond that was a smooth, deep, swiftly flowing sheet of water that swept past the willows at the bend and ended in a quarter of a mile of rough, turbulent water, rapids and falls.

"I'm going to help him!" exclaimed **Frank,** suddenly.

He stopped on the bank and flung off his coat, then started to untie his shoelaces in order to kick his light shoes aside.

But in the meantime Joe had managed to catch at a projecting rock with his free hand, so Chet put a restraining hand on Frank's arm.

For a moment it seemed that the current would make Joe lose his grip, but he clung to

the rock and drew himself closer until he had
wrapped his arm about it. The rest of the rock
was wide and flat and lay just a few inches
beneath the surface.

Slowly, Joe clambered on to this precarious
refuge, dragging the half-conscious boy with
him. The rock was big enough to provide foot-
hold for them both.

The boy was unable to help himself, as he was
limp and weak from his experience. Just as
he was almost on the rock Joe lost his grip on
the lad's collar for a second, and the current
whirled him to one side. The lad toppled backward, striking his head on the rock, but Joe
made a frantic grab for him, at imminent
risk of precipitating himself into the water
again.

His fingers closed about the back of the lad's
shirt and he managed to haul the boy to safety
once more.

But the blow had rendered the lad unconscious. He lay limply on the flat rock, with
the water breaking about his body, while Joe,
his clothes drenched, clung to him.

"Get help! Get a rope!" Joe shouted, to
his companions on the bank.

Frank and Chet lost no time.

They fled back toward the old mill.

The affair in the river had passed unnoticed
by the millers, and when Chet and Frank

rushed up to the front door they found no one in sight.

"I'm going inside," declared Frank. "We'll have to get a rope or they'll be swept off that rock in no time."

The door was closed, but he pushed it open and entered the dim interior of the mill. But hardly had he stepped inside, with Chet at his heels, than he ran into the arms of one of the men whom he had seen outside the doorway some time previously.

"Hi, what do you want?" demanded the man angrily. He seized Frank by the shoulders and tried to push him back, out of the building. At the same time the other man came running out of a near-by door.

"What's going on here?" he shouted wrathfully. "What's all this about? Get out of here, you boys!"

The sound of voices evidently attracted the attention of a third man, for he, too, came running out of the shadows, carrying a heavy club, which he brandished threateningly.

"What do you want here?" he shouted excitedly. He was short and broad-shouldered, with a dirty kerchief knotted about his neck.

"We want a rope," Frank explained, taken aback by this hostile demonstration. "Your boy is drowning in the mill race!"

The three men became immediately concerned.  They crowded about, asking questions.

"What boy?"

"Where is he?"

"What do you want a rope for?"

"He fell into the river a few minutes ago. If we don't hurry he'll be drowned.  My brother rescued him and they're both on a rock down near the rapids," Frank said hurriedly.  "Get a rope—quick!"

"Get a rope, Markel!" shouted the bespectackled old man to the fellow with the club. "Hurry up!"

Markel dropped the club and ran back into the room from which he had come.  In a few moments he returned, dragging a lengh of stout rope.

"Where is he now?" asked the old man. "Lead the way."

The men of the mill had forgotten their first animosity when told of the plight of the boy, and now they followed Chet and Frank as the two boys ran outside again and raced along the bank to the place where the other boys were standing in an excited group, shouting advice and encouragement to Joe, who was still clinging to the rock.

Markel stumbled along the bank with the rope, and when he reached the group of boys they moved back to give him space.  He coiled the rope loosely in one hand, then whirled the free end of it about his head and flung it out into the stream.

But the rope fell short. Joe made a frantic grab for it, but Markel had misjudged the distance.

"Here—let me try it," demanded the oldest of the three men, pushing Markel impatiently to one side. He seized the loose end of the rope, drew the remainder of it from the rushing water, then cast it out to Joe.

The rope whirled through the air, missed Joe's outstretched fingers by inches, then splashed into the water.

Again the old man drew the rope back, again he swung it about his head and again it arched out above the river.

This time it fell against Joe's shoulders. The youth, still clinging to the unconscious form on the rock, hastily grabbed at it, seized it, and began hastily tying it about his shoulders, underneath his arms.

He was handicapped by the fact that he had but one arm free, but at last he had the rope securely knotted.

The old man was greatly excited. He had noticed that boy the had not moved and that Joe had to cling to him to keep him from being swept off the rock.

"Lester!" he shouted. "Lester! Are you all right?"

"He hit his head on a rock and it knocked him out," explained Jerry. "I don't think he's badly hurt."

At that moment Joe looked up and waved to them, as a signal that they could begin towing him ashore. He tightened his hold on the unconscious boy, then eased himself off the rock.

The old man, Frank and Markel seized the end of the rope, and as Joe released his hold of the rock they began to pull.

The rope was an old one and Frank noticed, with alarm, that it was worn and frayed. Would it hold?

The figures in the water bobbed up and down in the waves, sometimes submerged completely. Bit by bit, they were drawn toward the bank.

But their combined weight and the strength of the current proved too much for the rope.

When they were but a few yards from shore the rope abruptly snapped.

The men and the boys on the bank staggered back as the loose end of the rope spun through the air.

Joe and Lester were swept away in the swift current!

# CHAPTER IX

## The Rescue

Frank Hardy had seen that the rope was insecure. He had already laid a plan of action in case the rope broke.

The rapids were just around the bend in the river. The stream was narrow at that point and willow trees overhung the bank. The moment the rope broke Frank leaped into action.

He stumbled free of the group and raced along the river bank toward the willows. He could see Joe struggling helplessly in the swiftly flowing stream and he knew that if the current once carried him beyond the willows his brother would be doomed. No human being could live in those tossing rapids.

Could he reach the trees in time? Would the current carry Joe and Lester close enough to the bank to enable him to rescue them? Would he be able to hold them until help arrived?

The bank suddenly dipped and he hurried down the grassy slope toward the willows. He was still in advance of the struggling figure in the stream and he knew that he had a chance, although it was but a slim chance at best, of rescuing his brother and the strange boy.

He reached the willows at last. They grew out over the smooth and rushing water. Frank ran to the edge of the soggy bank, grasped one of the trees, and leaned out over the stream.

So far, luck was with him, for Joe was still a few yards away. But he was still too far out in the water to enable Frank to grasp him as he passed.

But Joe had guessed Frank's intention. As well as he could, in spite of the fact that he was handicapped by the weight of the unconscious Lester, he tried to struggle closer toward the shore.

The current was with him, for it swung close to the bend at this point and it swept Joe directly beneath the overhanging willow to which Frank was clinging, steadying himself with his feet on the bank.

As Joe was swept beneath him, Frank reached far down. For one breathless second he thought he had missed his brother's outstretched hand. Then their fingers met and he gripped Joe tightly, hanging on to him with all his strength.

The willow bent and swayed beneath the added weight, but Frank held firm. The muscles of his arm ached with the strain and he knew that he could not hold out long, but already he could hear shouts and the sounds of running feet that told him the others were coming to the rescue.

"Hang on! We're coming!" Chet was shouting, and a moment later Frank heard his chum threshing through the bushes. Phil and the others were close behind.

With his companions clinging to him, Frank managed to drag Joe ashore, still grasping the clothes of the unconscious boy. Dripping wet, Joe scrambled up on the bank, and together they carried Lester out of the willows on to the grass.

First aid was immediately rendered. Lester was not seriously hurt. He had swallowed a great quantity of water and the blow on the head had stunned him, but after a while he stirred and opened his eyes. The old man looked relieved, although the other two men watched the scene with indifference.

When Lester was finally able to sit up his first question was.

"Who saved me?"

Frank indicated his brother.

"Joe did."

Lester struggled to his feet and gratefully shook Joe's hand.

"I don't know how to thank you," he said

simply. "But you know I'm grateful. I would have been drowned if it hadn't been for you."

Joe was embarrassed.

"It was him, really," he said, indicating Frank. "If it hadn't been for him we'd have both been in the rapids by now."

Lester grasped Frank by the hand.

"I have both of you to thank, then. You risked your lives for me."

The old man nodded.

"It was brave work," he said reluctantly. "I'm mighty thankful to you boys for saving the lad. And after this," he said harshly to Lester, "stay away from that mill race. I've told you fifty times that you're liable to get drowned fooling around there. Next time you mightn't be so lucky."

"I'm sorry, Uncle Dock," answered the boy.

The party made their way back toward the mill and the boys were conscious of the sullen glances of the two men who were with "Uncle Dock." It was clear that the pair wished the lads would go away.

"Better take the kid inside and let him dry his clothes," advised Markel roughly, gesturing to Lester. "We'd better get back to work."

Joe's clothes were soaked, but the offer evidently did not include him.

"Have you got a fire in the mill?" he hinted hopefully.

Uncle Dock glanced at Markel, who shook his head in a surly manner.

"No," he answered. "Lester can go to bed until his clothes dry."

"My own clothes are pretty wet."

Markel affected not to hear this remark, but hastened on toward the mill.

"When did you take over the mill?" asked Frank of the old man.

"A few weeks ago."

"What are your prices for milling?" asked Chet. "My father was saying the other day that he wished the old Turner mill would open again. If he had known you were running the place he would have been over by now. He can put a lot of trade your way."

Uncle Dock hesitated and glanced at the other man.

"You'd better talk to him, Kurt."

"Our prices are pretty high," said Kurt shortly. "We're makin' breakfast foods, chiefly."

"But don't you need grain?"

"We're pretty well stocked up."

"What are your milling prices, anyway?" persisted Chet.

Kurt thought for a moment, then gave Chet a list of prices which were so greatly in excess of those charged by the Bayport mills that they were prohibitive.

"Why, that's higher than dad would want to pay," Chet said.

Uncle Dock shrugged his shoulders.

"Take it or leave it. We ain't askin' for his trade."

"You won't get it. Not at those prices."

It was quite evident that Uncle Dock and his strange associates were not desirous of encouraging any outside trade for the old mill. However, Frank realized that the men had a right to manufacture patented food in secret if they wished, so he nudged Chet as a signal against any further questions.

They had reached the door of the mill by now, and Markel hustled Lester inside before he had a chance to say anything further to the boys, although the lad cast an appealing glance behind as though he would have liked again to express his thanks to his rescuers.

"Where do you fellows live?" asked Kurt, peering at them from under his shaggy eyebrows.

"Bayport."

"You're a long way from home."

"We're just on a hike," explained Frank. "We just thought we'd come around this way."

"You'll be late for supper if you don't hurry back."

This broad hint was not lost on the boys.

It was clear that the men wanted to get rid of them.

"I guess we'll be on our way. We'll go in for a swim farther up the river so Joe can have a chance to dry his clothes."

This seemed to remind Uncle Dock of the fact that Joe had, after all, saved Lester's life. He reached for his pocket.

"I'd like to reward you for saving the lad," he said, becoming suddenly affable. Joe shook his head, and when Uncle Dock took two five dollar bills from his pocket and offered them to the boys, one to Frank and the other to Joe, they disclaimed any intention of accepting money for what had plainly been their duty.

But no sooner had Uncle Dock extended the bills than the other man, Kurt, gave a muffled exclamation and stepped forward. He snatched the money from Uncle Dock's hands and quickly turned around, with his back to the boys.

The interruption was only of about a second's duration, for Kurt at once wheeled about and again extended the money. He gave a short, nervous laugh.

"My mistake!" he said. "I thought he was only offering you a dollar each. You deserve five. It's all right. Here—take it."

He thrust the money upon them but they refused. Kurt did not press the point. He put the bills back in his own pocket.

"All right. If you won't, I suppose there's no use arguing," he said, with evident relief. "But we're very grateful to you just the same. Well, Dock, what say we get back to work?" he continued, turning to his companion.

Uncle Dock turned away and went back into the mill with Kurt.

"It's plain they don't want *us* hanging around," said Joe, with a rueful glance at his clothes. "Let's go on up the river so I can throw these clothes over a hickory limb and get 'em dried out before we start back home."

# CHAPTER X

## The New Boat

A week went by, a week in which the Hardy boys and their chums again wrestled with refractory Latin phrases and geometrical problems, as the examinations drew near. There was little time for fun, even outside school hours. The boys were all overcome by that helpless feeling that comes with the approach of examinations, the feeling that everything they had ever known had somehow escaped their memory and that as fast as they learned one fact they forgot another.

But the week was over at last and on Saturday morning Fenton Hardy looked up from his newspaper with a quiet smile.

"What's the program for to-day?" he asked of his sons.

"Nothing in particular," said Frank. "I was thinking I'd dig into the Latin for an hour or so, although I'm so sick of the sight of that book that I'd like to throw it out the window."

"I'm away behind in my algebra," spoke up

Joe. "But it's too nice a day to study. Anyway, I've been working hard all week."

"Perhaps if you went down to the boathouse you might find something there," suggested their father casually.

The boys stared incredulously. Then they gave a simultaneous whoop of delight.

"You don't mean to say the motorboat is here?" exclaimed Frank.

Their father had taken charge of the buying of the motorboat for them. They had not expected that the craft would arrive until the start of the summer holidays.

Fenton Hardy merely smiled and turned to the financial page.

"It mightn't be a bad idea to go down to the boathouse anyway," he said.

The boys needed no further urging. Within a few seconds they were scrambling for their caps, within the minute they were racing down the front steps, and soon they were hastening toward Barmet Bay.

In preparation for the arrival of the motorboat they had rented a boathouse on the southern shore of the bay, at the foot of the street on which they lived. During the week, Mr. Hardy had obtained the key from them on some pretext, but they had thought nothing of it. Now everything was clear.

"The boat must have arrived here during

the week and he had it taken to the boathouse without telling us about it," said Frank.

"I guess he was afraid we wouldn't do much studying for the rest of the week if we knew it was there."

"I guess we wouldn't have, either."

When they reached the boathouse they could hardly contain themselves in their eagerness to see if the boat had indeed arrived. Frank inserted the key in the lock and opened the door. They stepped inside.

There, rocking gently in the waves, was a long, graceful craft, white with gilt trimmings, a motorboat that gave an immediate impression of strength and power without the sacrifice of graceful lines. There was a flag at the bow and at the stern; the fittings glistened; the seats were upholstered in leather, and across the bow was the name of the boat in raised letters: *SLEUTH*. The named had been chosen by the Hardy boys previous to the purchase of the craft and after much argument.

"She's a beauty!" breathed Frank in deep admiration.

"I'll say!"

"The smoothest looking boat on the bay!"

"And I'll bet it's the fastest."

"Oh, boy, if we'd only known this was here all week!"

Without further ado, the boys descended

from the landing stage and got into the boat to inspect the craft more closely. Everything they saw only served to confirm their first impression that the *Sleuth* was without doubt the neatest, most compact and most beautiful motorboat ever launched. The fittings were bright and shining, the wheel responded to the lightest touch.

"How's the gas and oil?" asked Frank, settling into the steersman's seat.

"Full up. And look, Frank, even the license is here!"

"All right. Cast off."

Joe opened the boathouse doors, unhooked the chains that kept the craft secure, and then leaped into the *Sleuth* as the engine spluttered and roared. Frank threw in the clutch, the roar died away to a purr, and the boat backed swiftly and smoothly out into the bay.

"The engine runs like a watch!" reported Frank, in delight.

Once outside the boathouse he headed the craft out toward the open bay. It was soon apparent that the engine of the *Sleuth* was very powerful, for the boat leaped forward as Frank increased speed, and yet there was very little noise. The nose of the boat cut the water like a knife and the craft skimmed out into the bay like a swallow.

Both boys were almost inarticulate with delight. The sense of speed and freedom held them spellbound. Frank changed places with Joe and gave his brother a turn at the wheel. Joe was astonished at the immediate response that came to his lightest touch.

In anticipation of getting the boat both lads had taken lessons in running such a craft from Tony Prito and others who had motor-boats and, as a consequence, Joe and Frank felt thoroughly at home with both the engine and the steering wheel.

They circled about and came down toward shore again. It was a sunny morning and two or three motorboats were spluttering and back-firing in their shelters near the shore. Out of one boathouse came a rakish black craft that the boys recognized instantly as the motor-boat belonging to Tony Prito's father.

"There's Tony!" exclaimed Frank. "He always goes boating on Saturday mornings. Let's give him a race."

"His boat's supposed to be the fastest on the bay."

"I don't care whether it is or not. He'll have to go some to beat the *Sleuth*. We'll challenge him."

Although Tony had seen their boat he had not yet recognized the boys in it and when they drew alongside he gave a shout of surprise.

"Well, gee whiz!" he exclaimed. "Look who's here! I was wondering who owned the swell new tub. Is this the new boat?"

"This is she. And she's fast, boy—she's fast. Want to race?"

Tony laughed.

"I hate to show you up so soon. You won't like your new boat near so well if I beat you the first time you get into a race."

"You won't beat us. You've got a pretty speedy old boat there, all right, but you've met your match this time."

"Do you really think you can lick me?" asked Tony. "You know you haven't a chance. This is a *real* speed boat."

"This is a better one. Come on—we'll start from that buoy."

Frank pointed to a buoy that was riding the waves about a hundred yards away and the two boats sped toward it. They kept on even terms until they came abreast of the buoy and then Tony shouted:

"Now!"

At the same instant, the boats leaped forward. The engine of Tony's craft set up a deafening roar, but the *Sleuth* merely changed from a purr to a growl and sprang swiftly through the water.

Tony had the advantage in that he knew his boat well and he knew just how much power it would stand. Within half a minute he had established a substantial lead, while the *Sleuth* was surging along in his wake.

But Frank knew that the boat was more powerful than it seemed.

Gradually, he "let her out," and the *Sleuth* responded until at last he could see that they were gaining on the craft ahead. By this time Tony was tearing along at the highest speed of which his swift craft was capable, and the boat was almost rising out of the water with the force of its momentum.

Rapidly, the *Sleuth* overhauled the flying craft, swiftly it drew abreast, and the boys had a glimpse of Tony's astonished face as he glanced over the side at them.

The *Sleuth* roared on, rocking and swaying, with spray dashing over the bows. There was no doubt as to which was the swifter craft. Tony was being left behind.

When a gap of three or four hundred yards separated the two boats and when it was apparent that he had no hope of overhauling his rival, Tony lessened the speed of his craft as a signal that he had been beaten. Frank immediately throttled down the *Sleuth* and swung her around in a wide circle. Then, at a more reasonable speed, they went back to meet Tony.

Their chum was astonished beyond all measure.

"I thought you were just kidding when you said you'd race with me," he shouted, as they drew closer.

"No kidding about that race, was there?"

"I'll say there wasn't! I let my old boat out as fast as she'd go. I thought the engine was going to jump out, once or twice. I didn't think there was a motorboat in the bay could beat mine, but I guess that tub of yours has it beat. When did you get it?"

"This is the first time we've been out."

"Wish I could stick around and race with you again," said Tony regretfully. "But I have to go back to the boathouse. I promised my father I'd help him at the warehouse this, morning."

"Tough luck," sympathized Frank. "We may see you this afternoon. But no more racing until the engine is worked in a bit better. It was foolish to let her out while she is so stiff."

"Where are you going now?"

"Oh, we'll just cruise around," said Frank. "I was thinking we might go up to Barmet village and back."

"That's a nice run. It'll take you about half an hour if you go easy. About five minutes if you let that speed demon out for all she's worth."

"We'll go easy," laughed Joe. "We don't

want to ruin the engine on our first trip.''
"Runs pretty smooth," approved Tony.
"It'll stand quite a lot. Well, I must be going.
Good-bye.''

He turned the nose of his craft toward the
boathouse and drew swiftly away. The Hardy
boys set out in the opposite direction, surging
through the water toward Barmet village.

# CHAPTER XI

## A Man in a Hurry

Barmet village lay several miles from Bayport on the shore of Barmet Bay, from which it got its name. It was a small place, inhabited by fishermen chiefly, and it was a distributing center for the farmers who lived in the surrounding area. The Hardy boys had no particular object in going to Barmet, beyond the fact that the village served as a destination and gave their boating trip more of a purpose than there would have been had they merely cruised aimlessly around.

Although the sky had been clear and the sun had been shining when they set out, Frank noticed that already clouds were coming in from the sea and the wind was stiffening. Storms sprang up suddenly along the coast but he was not alarmed for he knew that they would have the wind with them on the return trip.

The *Sleuth* sped smoothly along, the engine purring without a miss. The craft neither rocked nor rolled, but cut the waves cleanly.

Both Frank and Joe were delighted beyond measure with their boat, and at that moment would not have traded places with a king.

By the time they reached Barmet, the sky was cloudier than ever and there was a hint of rain, so the boys determined that they would not stay long in the village. They made a landing at the wharf and got out to stretch their legs, being greatly pleased in the meantime by the complimentary remarks passed by such villagers as were about at the time, on the appearance of their boat.

These were not empty compliments, for the Barmet people prided themselves on knowing a good boat when they saw one and there was nothing grudging in their approval of the *Sleuth*. Two old fishermen sat on the wharf with their feet dangling over the water and discussed the motorboat in every detail from bow to stern, agreeing that she combined strength and appearance in a remarkable degree. When they had finally affixed their seal of approval to the *Sleuth* they refilled their pipes and settled down to an endless series of reminiscences concerning boats that they had once sailed.

"The sky's beginning to look black," pointed out Frank to his brother after they had listened to a number of these tales. I guess we'd better be starting."

Joe moved away reluctantly, for he was fascinated by the highly colored yarns of the two old salts. But when he glanced at the lowering horizon he realized that Frank's apprehensions were justified and that it would be better for them to start back to Bayport without delay.

They got into the boat and were just about to cast off when there came a sudden interruption.

A man came running down the road leading to the dock. He was waving his arms and shouting.

"Hi! Hey there! Wait for me?"

Somewhat puzzled, the Hardy boys waited. They did not recognize the man; he was a complete stranger to them. He was stout and thick-set, florid of face and red of hair, and as he ran out on the wharf he panted from his exertions.

"Whew!" he exclaimed, mopping his brow with a bright silk handkerchief. "I nearly missed you."

"What do you want?" Frank asked.

"I wanted to go to Bayport—right away. I want to catch that train, and if you can get me there in twenty minutes I'll give you ten dol-lars. Will you take me?"

The Hardy boys looked at one another doubtfully. Both were conversant with the

Bayport train schedules and neither was aware
of any train that left Bayport at that hour in
the morning. Still, the stranger seemed very
much in earnest and he drew a ten dollar bill
from his pocket as proof of his good faith.

"Come!" he said impatiently. "How about
it? Will you take me or will you not? I want
to be there in twenty minutes. There's ten
dollars in it for you."

Ten dollars, as Frank said later, "is not to
be sneezed at." When they bought the motorboat their father made the stipulation that
they should not draw on their bank accounts to
pay for the gasoline, and every cent was precious for that reason.

"Jump in," Frank said. "I guess we can
get you there in twenty minutes, all right."

"Thanks," said the florid-faced man, getting
into the boat. "Make it as quick as you can."

Frank slipped into his seat and in a few moments the engine was roaring as the *Sleuth*
glided away from the shadow of the wharf
and headed out into the bay. She rapidly
picked up speed and soon the salt spray was
flying as the motorboat tore through the waves,
her nose pointing toward Bayport.

The stranger settled back with a sigh of
relief.

"Mighty good thing I met you," he said. "I
was beginning to think I wouldn't be able to

get out at all. There was only a rickety look-ing flivver in the village and I was afraid to take a chance on it, for I don't think it would have lasted a mile without falling to pieces. It was lucky I saw your boat when I did."

The *Sleuth* sped along under a darkening sky. They were running close to the shore in order to cut off as much distance as possible and keep a bee line for Bayport, and it was possible to have a clear view of the road that ran just above the beach.

Joe noticed that the stranger cast frequent anxious glances toward the shore. Suddenly an expression of alarm crossed the man's face, and Joe saw that he was watching two figures who had appeared on the road and who were running along, waving their arms, evidently trying to attract attention.

"Somebody signaling to us," he said to Frank.

Frank looked up. The two men on the road were making frantic efforts to draw attention, as they waved their arms and leaped about like lunatics.

"Friends of yours?" asked Frank of their passenger.

The florid-faced man laughed. The laugh was meant to be carefree and hearty, but there was no disguising the note of uneasiness be-neath it.

"Yes—yes, they're friends of mine," he admitted. "I put one over on them that time." He chuckled nervously. "They're just beginning to realize that I've given them the slip."

"What's the big idea?"

"That's the time I fooled them." The stranger laughed loudly—too loudly, in fact. "You see, I'm going to be married. That's why I have to catch that train. I kept it a secret until this morning, but my friends got wind of it and thought they'd play a practical joke on me. I started out in plenty of time for the train, but they had fixed the engine of my car so it broke down and I had to come back to Barmet. They were trying to hold me back, and for a while I was beginning to think that they had got away with it. But I bested 'em. I fooled 'em that time."

He laughed again, but still there was that note of insincerity in his mirth that had aroused the suspicions of the Hardy boys at first. They said nothing, and the stranger evidently thought his story had been believed, for he sat back in the boat with a complacent air.

But Frank glanced again at the two men on the road. For practical jokers, they seemed to be making a tremendous fuss over their friend's escape. They were still waving their arms, evidently trying to signal to the boat to turn back.

"There's something fishy about this," muttered Frank. "I don't know of any train leaving Bayport at this hour of the day."

"Neither do I," his brother replied, in a low voice.

"Those men on the shore seem mighty agitated over something or other. If it was a practical joke they'd just give up and go back to the village."

"It's a pretty queer story. He seemed in an awful hurry to get away from Barmet."

"I have a good mind to turn back. We may be getting ourselves into trouble."

"He'll be as mad as hops if we do. Tell him we don't want his money, and take him back to Barmet."

The more Frank considered the situation the more he felt that the wisest course would be to turn back to Barmet and wash his hands of the whole affair. The stranger's story about an approaching wedding might be true and it might not, but there was the fact of which he was certain, that there was no train leaving Bayport at that hour of the day. He turned to the passenger.

"What time is your train leaving?"

"About ten-thirty."

"There's no train leaving Bayport at that time," said Frank flatly.

"That's the time my train leaves," insisted

the stranger, beginning to look somewhat flustered.

"The earliest train is at noon," put in Joe.

"I tell you, this train leaves at ten-thirty. I just have time to catch it."

"I'm afraid you're going to miss it," said Frank. "I'm going to turn back to Barmet."

"Turn back?" shouted the man in consternation. "What are you going to do that for?"

"I don't like the looks of this affair," said Frank. "Considering that this is supposed to be nothing more than a practical joke, those two men on shore seem to be making quite a fuss over your escape."

"They're hoping they can persuade you to turn back. Then they'll have the joke on me after all."

"They're going to have it anyway," said Frank, with determination. "I've changed my mind about taking you to Bayport. We don't want your ten dollars."

"But you've *got* to take me to Bayport!" exclaimed the stranger, in high excitement. "I must catch my train."

His bullying manner nettled Frank.

"This is our boat, and if we want to turn back we can turn back," he told the passenger. "We didn't ask you to come with us."

"But you promised to take me to Bayport,"

stormed the stranger. "I've got to be there in time to catch that train."

"There isn't any train at ten-thirty, and we know it. We're going to turn back to Barmet and you'll have ample time to catch the noon train after that."

The stranger gritted his teeth and half rose from his seat. Then he sank back, as though realizing that he was going beyond his rights by objecting.

"A nice trick to play on me!" he snapped. "Bringing me this far and then turning back."

"Your friends on the shore seem anxious to have you back, for some reason or other."

Frank bore down on the wheel and the *Sleuth* slowly began to circle about.

Suddenly the voice of the stranger rasped right at their ears:

"Don't turn this boat around! Keep heading for Bayport."

Startled, they turned. The stranger was standing right behind them, and in his hand he clutched a revolver that was aimed directly at them!

# CHAPTER XII

## Seasick

The Hardy boys were not prepared for this sudden change of front on the part of the stranger. They gazed incredulously at the revolver, but the coldly determined face of their passenger convinced them that the man meant to use force if necessary.

"Keep right on toward Bayport!" he ordered. "Don't turn back."

"What's the big idea?" demanded Frank indignantly.

"The idea is that I want to go to Bayport, and if you won't take me there of your own free will, I'll just have to persuade you, that's all. This gun is loaded, so don't make any foolish moves."

The boys looked at one another, and the stranger began to chuckle.

"Be reasonable now," said the man with the gun. "I have to catch that train, or I'll miss the wedding. I can't let you bring me back to the village. My friends would never let me hear the end of that joke. It's just by luck I had this revolver in my pocket—but still, if you turn this boat around, I'll use it.''

He was trying to pass the affair off as more or less of a joke but there was no mistaking the steely glint in his eyes or the hardness of his voice.

Frank looked at his brother, and shrugged.

''I guess there's nothing else for it but bring him to Bayport,'' he muttered. ''I don't want to get shot.''

''That gun looks bad,'' agreed Joe. ''There's not much joking about that part of it.''

Frank bore down on the wheel and corrected the course of the boat so that they were soon bound directly for Bayport again.

''We'll take you to the city,'' he said to the stranger, ''but I'm going to warn you that we'll turn you over to the police if we get a chance. That's a dangerous game you're play-ing, even if you say it is only a joke. It's a hold up.''

''You'll think differently after we reach Bayport,'' promised the man. ''I'll have my wife write you a letter of thanks after the wed-ding. I hate to use this revolver, but I can't miss that train.''

The stranger's insistence on his story that he had to catch a train did not convince the

Hardy boys by any means. They were still suspicious of their passenger, the more so now that he used force to induce them to take him to Bayport.

"I'd like to get that gun away from him," whispered Frank, as he bent over the wheel.

"Not much chance. He's watching us too closely."

"Trying to fix up some plot to get hold of this revolver?" asked the stranger. "You needn't bother. I hold the whip hand here."

"We know it," retorted Frank. "But wait till we get to Bayport."

The motorboat raced on down the bay. The storm clouds that had been collecting all morning now hung heavily in the sky. The bay was sullen and slate-colored, and a heavy sea was running. White caps broke on the surface of the water.

"Looks like a storm," Frank muttered. "Perhaps it's just as well we didn't turn back."

A streak of lightning split the sky; it was followed by a distant rumble of thunder. The *Sleuth* was riding the waves well, but there was a rocking motion that could not be avoided. The boat swayed from side to side as it plunged on.

After about five minutes Frank glanced behind.

The stranger was no longer standing up; ne was sitting back against the cushions again and he still held the revolver levelled at the Hardy boys, but there was a curious expression on his face, an expression of nausea; his eyes were staring and his face was pallid.

For a moment Frank could not understand what the matter was. Then, as the boat gave a lurch more violent than usual, he understood.

He nudged his brother.

"Getting seasick!" he whispered.

Joe glanced back, and when he saw that the stranger's florid face had changed in hue from a deep red to a greenish white he knew that the motion of the boat was indeed taking its effect. He forebore an impulse to chuckle at their passenger's plight.

"Give her a little more gas," ordered the stranger, in a curiously feeble voice. "You're not going fast enough."

He brandished the revolver threateningly.

Frank obligingly increased the speed of the *Sleuth* but the rocking motion only became more pronounced.

The stranger gulped, but he did not lower the weapon.

"That's better," he said, without enthusiasm.

"I'm going to give him something to be seasick about," whispered Frank.

Without warning he suddenly bore down on the wheel and swung the motorboat about so that it was lying broadside to the waves.

"Here—what's the matter?" asked the stranger. "Where are you going now?"

"We're off our course. I'm heading in toward shore a little more so we can get out of the wind."

This explanation satisfied the stranger, although it became speedily apparent that the new course did not.

The *Sleuth* received the full force of the long rollers. The waves were not high enough to be dangerous, but the swells gave an undulating motion to the craft that swiftly increased the stranger's illness.

"He's slipping," whispered Joe.

Frank glanced back again.

The stranger was indeed "slipping." He teeth were tightly clenched. His face was almost green. His expression was that of a man who is deathly sick. But he still clung to the revolver and he still waved it feebly at the boys.

"Head her in toward Bayport," he demanded. "Do you want to make me sick?"

"This'll fix him," said Frank. "Get ready."

He bore down on the wheel again.

The *Sleuth* swung around at right angles to

her previous course. The abrupt, swerving motion finished the stranger.

With a groan, he slumped forward in his seat, and bowed his head on his arms.

Joe sprang up. With one bound he reached the man with the gun.

The stranger realized what was happening, and struggled to his feet. He raised the weapon, but Joe struck out and dashed the revolver from his hand. It described a flashing arc, then fell into the water with a splash.

Sick as he was, the man swung out viciously and his fist caught Joe on the side of the face, staggering him. Joe quickly recovered himself and plunged forward, grappling with the man. They swayed to and fro in the middle of the boat, then fell, still struggling.

But although Joe was young and wiry he was not strong enough to cope with his antagonist and Frank soon saw that the stranger was having the better of the battle. He glanced ahead, saw that the *Sleuth* was heading into a long, low bank of fog but that there were no other boats in sight, then abandoned the wheel.

He leaped back to the assistance of his brother, crooked his elbow about the stranger's neck, and dragged him back. The man struck out, wildly, twisted around and staggered Frank with a blow in the ribs. He managed to struggle to his feet, they saw his hand flash to his pocket, and then he produced a small package and flung it far out over the side.

It had only taken a second, but that second was sufficient to serve for his undoing.

Frank scrambled to his feet in the swaying boat, and for a moment they sparred. Then Frank's right fist shot out and the blow landed directly on the point of the stranger's jaw.

The man was not knocked out, but he staggered back and the wild lurching of the boat sent him off his balance. He stumbled and fell. His head struck against the side of the boat and he crumpled up in a heap.

The blow had knocked him unconscious.

Frank bent over him. He saw that the man was not badly hurt, but that he had been stunned by the impact. He pointed out a coil of rope in the stern.

"Tie his ankles, Joe, in case he wakes up. I've got to get back to the wheel."

The *Sleuth* by this time was off her course, and was wallowing in the trough of the waves. Quickly, Frank swung the craft about, but when he peered ahead to locate Bayport he gave an exclamation of alarm.

The city was nowhere to be seen. The heavy cloud of mist that had been gathering over the bay now totally obscured the shores.

How far the boat had departed from her

course he did not know, and in the fog bank he had but a vague idea of their location. He began to look around in hopes of finding a compass, but there was none in the boat.

"Have you got a pocket campass, Joe?"

Joe, who was busily engaged in tying the unconscious stranger's ankles together, looked up and shook his head.

"Isn't there one in the boat?"

"No—and here we are in a fog bank. I don't know whether we're in the right direction for Bayport or not."

## CHAPTER XIII

### PAUL BLUM

FRANK HARDY reduced the speed of the motorboat, because he realized the dangers that lurked in the fog.

Almost any moment they might crash into another boat in the bay. Even worse, they might be so far out of their course that they would pile up on one of the rocky shores.

The fog was impenetrable. Frank did his best to judge their direction by the waves but this did not help greatly, as there were cross currents and the wind was shifting.

The *Sleuth* coursed on, feeling its way blindly through the haze that enveloped the bay. Frank peered ahead into the foggy veil.

Joe concluded his ministrations to the stranger, who was now beginning to stir. The man opened his eyes and groaned.

"Have you had enough?" asked Joe.

"Who hit me?"

"You hit your head against the side of the

boat.   Are you going to make any more trouble?''

The man groaned again, tried to get to his feet, found that his ankles were tied together, and sank back with a sigh.

''He won't give us any more bother,'' declared Joe, coming forward.   It was plain that there was no more fight left in their captive.

''I wish this fog would lift,'' said Frank.

As though in answer to his words a sudden gust of wind sent the mist in scurrying wreaths, raising the heavy grey veil long enough to enable him to see Bayport lying almost directly ahead.   He could make out the position of the row of boathouses and he headed the *Sleuth* toward them.

The curtain of fog descended again, but Frank was now fairly sure of his position.

''We're heading in the right direction now.''

''Should we try to make the boathouse?   I don't think we'll be able to find it in this mist.''

''I guess you're right.   We'll land at the big wharf.''

In a short while, the boat was nosing its way through the fog, among the shadowy craft anchored near Bayport wharf.   The city loomed up in a ghostly dark mass beyond the water.

Finally the *Sleuth* drew alongside the wharf

and nosed its way to one of the slips. To the surprise of the boys they saw several figures running along the wharf.

"What boat is that?" shouted some one from the fog.

"The *Sleuth!*"

"Good! That's them. I thought they'd land here," said the voice, evidently addressing some one else on the wharf.

"Looks as if we're expected," observed Joe.

A man came down the slip, and even in the fog they knew the figure was familiar. When he drew closer they saw that the man was none other than their father.

"Dad!" exclaimed Frank.

"Have you got him with you?" asked the detective quickly.

"Who? Joe?"

"No, no. The man you picked up at Barmet village. I had a telephone message about him."

"Yes, we have him here. He tried to hold us up with a revolver, but we got the better of him."

"Fine!" said Mr. Hardy, peering down into the boat, where the stranger was struggling to sit up. "All right, Chief!" he called, to a burly man who has coming down the slip. "They have him."

Chief Collig, of the Bayport police force, and

Con Riley, one of his men, then appeared in view.

"Got him, hey?" said Collig.

"They have him here in the boat."

"All right. Hand him over."

Still wondering how their father had known that the stranger was in the boat with them and wondering also why the police were on hand, the Hardy boys untied the ropes that bound their passenger's ankles, and helped him over the side. He was immediately seized by the officers, who proceeded to search his pockets.

"Here!" he protested. "What's all this about?"

"Well, Paul Blum," said Fenton Hardy, "you thought you'd made a getaway, didn't you?"

The man started.

"You have my name wrong," he muttered.

"Oh, no, I haven't," contradicted Mr. Hardy. "They tell me you were 'shoving the queer' down in Barmet village this morning."

The Hardy boys had been told by their father that 'shoving the queer' was the underworld expression for passing counterfeit money.

"Those Secret Service men would have caught you if the boat hadn't been handy,"

went on Fenton Hardy. He turned to his sons:
"What sort of story did this fellow tell you?"

"He said he had to catch a train, as he was
going to be married, and some of his friends
in the village were trying to hold him back, as
a practical joke," answered Frank. "We
thought the yarn was rather fishy and I was
going to turn back but he drew a revolver on
us."

"How did you get him tied up?"

"He got seasick and Joe knocked the gun
out of his hand. Then we tackled him."

"Good work," approved Mr. Hardy. "I got
a 'phone call from two Secret Service men this
morning. It seems they've been trailing Paul
Blum for some time and they were just about
to arrest him when he made a bolt for liberty.
They chased him down the street, but he dis
appeared, and the next thing they knew he was
in your boat, heading for Bayport. They
waved at you and tried to signal to you to come
back—"

"So that's why the two fellows were running along the shore!" exclaimed Joe.

"But when you didn't turn back they tele-
phoned to me to meet the boat and arrest him."
Fenton Hardy turned to Chief Collig. "Did
you find anything?" he asked.

The Chief straightened up, scratching his
head.

"Not a thing. Nothin' but a dollar bill and some matches."

"No counterfeit money?" exclaimed Mr. Hardy, in surprise.

"Not a bit."

"That's strange. The detectives told me he had a big roll of bad bills."

"Why, that must have been what he threw overboard," said Frank. "He took something out of his pocket and tossed it over the side of the boat while we were fighting with him. At the time I couldn't imagine what it was."

"I guess that's how he got rid of it." Fenton Hardy turned to Paul Blum, who was standing sullenly, with his pockets turned inside out. "And what have you got to say for yourself, Blum?"

"Nothing. You haven't got anythin' against me."

"Perhaps not just now. But wait till those Secret Service men arrive from Barmet. You were passing counterfeit money in the village."

"Any counterfeit money I passed, I got from some one else," blurted the prisoner. "I'm not in that game."

Fenton Hardy turned to his sons.

"This doesn't happen, by any chance, to be the fellow who tricked you on that bad five dollar bill at the railway station, does it?" he asked.

They shook their heads.

"No, it isn't he."

"I'm convinced that he's associated with the gang in some way."

"You haven't got anything on me," Blum persisted doggedly. "Perhaps I did pass some bad money in the village. What of it? If I did, I didn't know it was bad. I got it from some one else. It ain't my fault."

"If you're so innocent, why did you run from the detectives?"

"I had to catch a train."

"Tell that to the judge," advised Chief Collig roughly. "I think I'll lock you up for a while, my friend, and let you just think things over."

"Yeh, put him in the cooler," piped up Con Riley.

"I don't want any advice from you," said the chief, crushing his subordinate officer with a frown. "Here—put the cuffs on this bird and lock him up."

There was a jingle of handcuffs as they were clapped about Paul Blum's wrists. The man protested, but he was quickly silenced by the chief.

"We're going to keep you until the Secret Service men get here," said Fenton Hardy. "Perhaps they'll have more to tell."

Chief Collig and Constable Riley trudged

off, with Paul Blum between them. Fenton Hardy turned to his sons with a smile of approval.

"Good work!" he said. "You haven't lost any time making good use of the new boat, I see."

"I only wish we could have got hold of that roll of counterfeit bills he threw overboard," said Frank disconsolately.

"Well, it can't be helped now—although that would have cinched the case against Blum. He has been operating in this neighborhood for over a week. But I expcet the Secret Service men will have enough evidence to have him punished."

The fog was beginning to lift and the Hardy boys had no further doubt of their ability to locate the boathouse. They felt they had enough of motorboating for one morning, so they said good-bye to their father and left the wharf, guiding the *Sleuth* safely to the boathouse.

"If every trip we have in the *Sleuth* is as exciting as that one, we'll have no reason to kick," Frank remarked, as he shut off the engine.

# CHAPTER XIV

## Con Riley Guards a Package

Officer Con Riley was at peace with the world.

His heart was full of contentment and his stomach was full of pie. The sun was shining and one of the aldermen had just given him a fairly good cigar. His beat had been free of crime for a week. His wife had gone to the country for a visit and she had taken the children with her. Hence, Con Riley's feeling of deep and lasting satisfaction with the world.

Even the boys, his natural and hereditary enemies, had not tormented him for several days. Perhaps, he argued, it was because they were up to their ears in work, preparing for examinations. If that was the reason, Con Riley decided that examinations were good things and should be encouraged.

As he sauntered along the shady side of Main Street, leisurely swinging his club and gravely responding to the greetings of, "Good afternoon, officer," he reflected that there were

worse occupations in life than being on the
Bayport police force. He was well content
with his lot just then. He exchanged saluta-
tions with the traffic cop on the main corner
and mentally congratulated himself because he
was not a traffic cop; the job exposed one to all
manner of weather, from cold, drenching rains
to sizzling heat. No, he was just as glad he
was on the beat.

A troop of boys came down the street from
the direction of the Bayport high school, and
Riley instinctively stiffened. If it were not for
those confounded boys, life would be very different for him. They did not seem to appre-
ciate the dignity of his position. They were
always contriving schemes to make him look
ridiculous.

He spied the Hardy boys with their companions, and his frown deepend. Too smart, altogether, those Hardy lads. They weren't
mischievous, he had to admit that, but they
were meddling in the work of the police a little
too much. Already they had been credited
with solving a couple of mysteries that he, Con
Riley, would certainly have solved alone if he
had been given a little more time.

Then there was Chet Morton—a boy who
was born to be hanged, if ever there was one.
He'd come to a bad end some day, that fellow.
So would all the rest of them, Tony Prito,

Phil Cohen, Jerry Gilroy, Biff Hooper—the whole pack of 'em.

Still, Con Riley was in a good humor that afternoon, so he unbended sufficiently to bestow a nod of greeting upon the boys. To his surprise they gathered around him.

"What has been done with Paul Blum?" asked Frank.

"He's in jail," said Riley, with the portentous frown he always assumed when discussing matters of crime. "He's in jail, and in jail he'll stay."

"Hasn't he been tried yet?"

The constable shook his head.

"Not yet. The rascal has a lawyer and the case has been adjourned."

"Not much doubt that he'll get a heavy sentence," remarked Chet, who was carrying beneath his arm a package wrapped in brown paper.

"No doubt of it at all," agreed Riley.

"Didn't you fellows tell me that Lieutenant Riley helped capture the counterfeiter?" asked Chet innocently, turning to the Hardy boys.

Riley's chest expanded visibly when he heard himself referred to as "Lieutenant," and when it dawned on him that Chet thought he had a part in the actual capture of Blum he tried to look as modest as possible, although he did not succeed very well.

"Oh, I helped. I helped," he said, with a deprecatory wave of the hand.

"If it hadn't been for Officer Riley the fellow might have got away," said Joe smoothly. "He slapped the handcuffs on Blum in the neatest manner you ever saw. He was waiting for us right at the dock."

Riley beamed. This was praise, however undeserved, and he basked in the admiration of the boys. He told himself that he had perhaps been mistaken in his estimation of these lads after all. They were not mischievous young rascals, but bright, intelligent, high-minded boys who recognized human worth when they saw it and who respected achieve-ment.

"Yes," he said heavily, "I got Blum behind the bars and he won't get out again in a hurry."

He said it as though he had personally been responsible for Blum's capture and personally responsible for seeing that the prisoner was kept safely locked up.

"No, he won't get away on you, Lieutenant Riley," said Chet.

Con Riley's opinion of Chet increased. The boy had mistaken him for a lieutenant. The mistake was natural enough, perhaps, but it would have to be corrected.

"Officer," he pointed out sadly. "Not lieutenant—officer."

"Do you mean to tell me that you're not a lieutenant?" exclaimed Chet in well-assumed amazement.

"Not yet," replied the officer, leaving the impression, however, that it was only a matter of hours before such promotion should be his in the natural course of events.

Chet turned to his companions.

"Can you imagine that!" he exclaimed. "There's the police force for you. They keep a solid, brainy man like Riley here on the beat and let fellows like Collig be chief. It's wrong, I tell you. It's wrong."

The boys gravely agreed that it was scandalous.

"A man's just got to be patient," said Riley, with the air of a martyr, and beginning to feel ill-used.

"There's a limit to patience!" exclaimed Chet. "They're imposing on you, Mr. Riley. If I were you, I'd insist on my rights."

"Never mind," said Riley darkly. "My turn will come."

"You're just right it will. And we'll see that it comes very soon. Let's try to stir up public opinion, fellows, and see if we can't influence the public a little bit. If the public demands that Officer Riley be promoted, he'll be promoted.''

''Why, that's very good of you,'' returned Riley pompously. ''A few words in the right place mightn't do any harm at all.''

''Those words shall be said,'' Chet assured him earnestly. ''You may depend on us, Mr. Riley. We will see that your qualities of leadership are recognized. You're the only man who can wake this city up.''

Con Riley, a trifle dazed by this avalanche of flattery, but nevertheless feeling that every bit of it was deserved and that the boys deserved credit for their perception, beamed with appreciation.

''Why, I never had no idea you lads felt like this,'' he said. ''I always thought you had a sort of grudge against me.''

The boys immediately disclaimed any such sentiments.

''We may have been a little bit troublesome at times,'' agreed Chet regretfully; ''but that was because we didn't understand you. After this, you may depend on us. Your time will come, Mr. Riley. Your time will come.''

With this fine oratorical effort, Chet produced the package from beneath his arm. ''By the way,'' he said, ''I wonder if you would mind guarding this package for me, Mr. Riley?

You'll be here for the next ten minutes, won't you?''

A doubt flashed across Riley's mind.

"Why don't your friends look after it?"

"We're all going to be together and we didn't care to wait. If a man by the name of Muggins comes along and asks for it, you'll give it to him, will you?"

Riley took the package. "I'll take care of it," he promised.

"I wouldn't trust it with any one but you," declared Chet solemnly.

"You can trust me. I'll look after it. And if your friend Muggins comes along I'll see that he gets it safely all right."

Chet thanked Riley warmly and the boys hastened off and disappeared around the next corner. Riley, with the package under one arm, leaned against a post and thought well of himself and of the world in general. He completely revised his opinions of boys, and particularly of Chet Morton, whom he now re-garded as an exceptionally intelligent lad who would make his mark in the world. Riley was glad that he was able to be of service to Chet by minding the package for him.

The package was not very heavy. Riley was curious as to its contents. Chet had left the impression that it contained something quite valuable. He said he would not trust any one but Riley to guard it. That, in itself, was a compliment.

The late afternoon was warm and as Con Riley leaned against the post and indulged in these pleasant meditations, permitting himself to speculate on what the boys had said about his fitness for promotion, allowing himself to remember how pleasant it had sounded to hear Chet refer to him as "Lieutenant," he became a bit drowsy. He was naturally a sleepy man, and he had long since schooled himself in the art of appearing to be wide awake while on duty while indulging in covert naps of a few minute's duration. The hurrying crowds of people behind him, because it was the five o'clock rush hour, gradually became a blurred impression of tramping feet and chattering voices.

Suddenly the shrill jangle of an alarm clock sounded.

Riley started violently, straightened up, blinked, and looked behind him.

The alarm clock trilled steadily. Riley looked suspiciously at the people near by and the people looked at one another. He looked up into the air, looked down at the pavement, but still the mysterious alarm clock rattled on.

Then Riley became aware that the alarm clock was in the package under his arm.

At the same time the crowd became aware of

the fact as well. Some one tittered; some one
else laughed outright.

"Carry your own alarm clock with you now,
do you?" asked a man.

Riley felt very foolish. He was tempted to
throw the package away, but instead he held it
gingerly by the string and pushed his way
through the crowd. The unremitting alarm
clock rang loudly.

"Time to wake up!" shouted a wit in the
crowd.

Riley flushed and hastened on down the
street. But the alarm clock shrilled relent-
lessly. That tinkling bell seemed as though
it would ring forever. And as Riley hurried
on his way people turned and stared and
laughed, and small boys began to follow him,
while all the time the bell trilled on without
a sign of weakening.

His journey down the street was a triumphal
procession. The crowd of small boys following him swelled to the proportions of a parade.
The bell rang on. Con Riley was the center
of interest. He did not know what to do. If
he threw away the package now it would be an
admission that he had been the victim of a
practical joke; the longer he kept the package
the more the crowd laughed and the louder the
bell seemed to ring.

His steps became faster and faster, as

though he were trying to run away from the sound. Every one was staring at him in amazement. The giggles and guffaws of the crowd became louder. The shouts of the small boys were more insistent.

Across Con Riley's mind flitted certain phrases of Chet Morton. "Your time will come. . . . You're the only man who can wake this city up. . . . We shall see that your qualities of leadership are recognized . . ."

With a mutter of wrath he flung the tinkling package into the nearest alley. A uniformed street cleaner who was just emerging from the alley received the package full in the chest and sat down very suddenly. He flung the package back at Riley. The crowd whooped with glee. The package fell into the street, the bell still ringing, and one of the small boys picked it up and ran after Riley, asking if he wanted it back.

Thus he was pursued to the police station until the bell of the alarm clock ceased to ring, and only then did the crowd scatter.

Mopping his brow, flushed with anger, Riley took refuge in the station and vowed vengeance in the future on all the boys in Bayport, particularly high school boys, most especially Chet Morton's gang, and most absolutely and positively Chet Morton himself.

As for that worthy, in company with his

chums, he had witnessed the alarm clock parade from a convenient corner across the street and was now limply making his way toward the Hardys' barn, pausing every now and then to burst into shrieks of laughter at the remembrance of Riley's undignified flight.

But when the Hardy boys and their chums reached the house they found their father hastening down the front steps.

"I just had a telephone message from the police station," he said.

"What's the matter?" asked Frank, while the other lads looked at one another guiltily. Had Riley reported them?

"Paul Blum has escaped from jail," said Fenton Hardy.

# CHAPTER XV

## THE CHASE

"WHEN?" asked the Hardy boys quickly, in response to their father's announcement of Paul Blum's escape.

"Just a few minutes ago. At least that was when they discovered it. He managed to get out into the jail yard for some exercise, and in some way the guard's attention was distracted. Blum piled up a couple of old boxes against the wall and was over before any one saw him."

"I wonder where he would go?"

"The police are watching the roads and the trains. I don't think he can get out of the city that way. But I have an idea he has accomplices here, and if he can he'll join them and they'll see that he is smuggled out all right. I was going to suggest that you fellows take the motorboat and keep an eye on the bay."

"Good idea!" exclaimed Frank, who never needed an excuse to take the boat out. "Come on, Joe. Come on, Chet."

"I'll go out in dad's boat," volunteered Tony Prito.

"Fine!" agreed the others, and the boys hastened down the street in the direction of the boathouses.

Jerry Gilroy and Biff Hooper went with Tony, while Phil Cohen went with Chet and the Hardy boys.

Frank unlocked the door of the boathouse and went inside, followed by the others.

But the familiar shape of the *Sleuth* could not be seen.

The front of the boathouse was open. The motorboat had disappeared.

"The boat's gone!" he exclaimed in consternation.

The other boys stared, amazed at this unexpected development.

"It's been stolen!" cried Frank. "No one has a key to the boathouse but Joe and me."

"It was here at noon!" exclaimed Joe. "I was in here for a few minutes before I went to school."

"Who could have taken it?" asked Chet.

"Do you think it could have been Paul Blum?" suggested Joe.

The same thought had been in Frank's mind.

"That's who it was! He wanted to make a quick getaway, so he figured his best chance would be by boat."

"And perhaps he found out where our boathouse was, just so he could get even because we turned him over to the police," Joe put in.

"He can't be very far away," Phil Cohen pointed out. "Your father said he just escaped a little while ago."

Frank ran along the landing out to the front of the boathouse. For a moment he scanned the bay. Then he gave a sudden shout.

"I see the boat! There's the *Sleuth!* I'd know it anywhere!"

The others ran to his side, and Frank pointed out a flashing white shape heading far up the bay. There were very few boats out that afternoon and there was no mistaking the *Sleuth* as it sped eastward.

"Get Tony to chase him!" exclaimed Joe. "Quick!"

They ran hurriedly out of the boathouse and made their way down to the ramshackle building where Tony Prito kept his craft. The other boys looked up in surprise as the Hardys and their companions entered. Tony had been just on the point of starting.

"Paul Blum has stolen our boat!" Frank told him. "He's making his getaway in it now!"

"Paul Blum!" exclaimed Tony.

"Yes. The escaped prisoner. There's the

boat now," declared Joe, as he pointed out toward the bay.

In a flash, Tony grasped the situation. He leaped into the motorboat.

"Jump in! We'll chase him."

The Hardy boys scrambled into the boat, but Chet and the others stayed behind.

"Too many cooks spoil the broth," explained Chet. "You'll need all the speed you can get out of that boat to catch him. We'd only delay you."

Chet was eager to join in the chase, but he realized that the fewer passengers Tony's boat carried, the better would be their chance of capturing the fugitive. The other boys quickly took their cue from his attitude and declared that they would remain behind also.

"We'll telephone to Barmet village," suggested Chet. "Perhaps a boat can put out from there and head him off."

His remarks were drowned in the roar of the engine, as Tony's motorboat began to back slowly out into deeper water. It left the boathouse, then Tony turned the wheel and the motorboat headed about for the open bay.

"Now I guess you wish the *Sleuth* wasn't faster than my boat," he said, with a grin. "We'll have trouble catching him."

He opened the throttle, and the motorboat

leaped ahead, leaving a widening trail of foaming water behind.

The white shape of the stolen craft could be seen far out in the bay. Paul Blum was losing no time, and it was evident that his method of escape had not yet been discovered by the police, as Tony's craft was the only boat in pursuit. It was doubtful, too, if the fugitive realized as yet that he was being pursued.

"I'll let her out as fast as she'll go," said Tony, suiting the action to the word.

The boat was drumming along at a high rate of speed and it soon became apparent that they were gaining on the *Sleuth*. This was evidently because Paul Blum thought his flight had passed unnoticed and did not feel it necessary to run the craft at its highest speed.

"If we can only sneak up behind him before he knows we're after him, we'll have a chance," said Joe.

"No such luck," Tony remarked. "He'll be looking behind once in a while."

Frank found a pair of binoculars on one of the seats, and he raised them to his eyes, adjusting them so that Paul Blum and the speeding motorboat were brought within his line of vision. The distant *Sleuth* leaped closer as he looked through the glasses, and he could

plainly see the face of the man at the wheel.
They had not been mistaken. The fugitive
was Paul Blum.

Even as Frank looked, the man turned, and
an expression of alarm crossed his face. He
had seen the motorboat pursuing him.

Frank saw Blum lean forward, and the
*Sleuth* began to increase its speed. The wing
of water cleft by its bow became higher and the
spray was flying. Swiftly, the motorboat began to draw away.

"He's seen us," said Frank, lowering the
binoculars.

"We'll keep after him, anyway."

"We'll chase him clean across the Atlantic
if the gas holds out," declared Tony.

Joe gave an exclamation of delight.

"The gas!" he exclaimed. "The gas!
That's where we have him. I went down to the
boathouse at noon just to see if there was
enough gas in the tank, and it's pretty low.
He hasn't enough to take him more than a few
miles."

"Good!" exclaimed Tony. "That's where
we have the edge. My boat may not be as fast
as the *Sleuth* but the gas tank's full and there's
some more in that can. We'll chase him till he
has to quit."

But if the gas in the *Sleuth's* tank was low,
there was no sign of it just then. The motor-

boat sped on up the bay, gradually widening the distance between itself and the pursuing craft. Tony crouched at the wheel, impassively watching the flashing white streak far ahead.

"I wonder where he's heading for," said Frank.

"Along the coast, probably," Tony answered. "He'll likely get out of the bay, then head up the coast as far as he can and abandon the boat."

"That's probably what he intends to do," put in Joe. "But he'll never get out of the bay. There isn't enough gas."

It was evident that Paul Blum had no intention of seeking refuge in Barmet village. On the contrary, he was heading toward the other side of the bay, in the direction of the mouth of Willow River.

"Perhaps he intends to go up the river," ventured Frank.

Tony shook his head.

"Not if he knows what's good for him. He'd run full plump into the falls and rapids near the old mill."

"That's right, too." Frank had forgotten those obstacles.

But while the *Sleuth* was still some distance away from the mouth of the river, her speed began to slacken.

"Good!" exclaimed Joe. "The gas tank's empty."

"Let us hope so," returned his brother. "What a sell for that man!"

But a moment later the other motorboat began to show signs of life again.

"She's started up!" groaned Joe. "Confound the luck, anyway."

A moment later a splutter came from the other boat.

"Gas must be running low," said Frank. "Gee, I wish he would stop entirely!"

"Same here."

Slower and slower went the white motorboat until at last it was just crawling along.

Frank picked up the binoculars again.

He could see Paul Blum laboring at the motor, trying to locate the source of trouble. The fugitive cast a glance backward; Frank could see the anxious expression on the man's face.

"He's trapped, and he knows it."

Rapidly, they gained on the *Sleuth*, which was now almost at a standstill, drifting back and forth in the waves. Paul Blum seized an oar that was carried in the boat in case of emergency, and frantically began to scull toward the shore.

But his effort was in vain. Tony's motorboat bore swiftly down upon him.  The engine of the *Sleuth* had died.

As the other craft drew alongside, Paul Blum cast aside the oar in admission of defeat. He sat sullenly in the boat without looking up.

"Too bad, Blum!" shouted Frank.  "We're going to take you back with us."

"I'd have been all right if it hadn't been for the confounded gas running out," gritted the man.

"We weren't so particular about getting you as we were about getting back our boat," said Joe.  "Will you come back quietly?"

Paul Blum shrugged his shoulders.

"I suppose I might as well," he said.  "I haven't any weapons.  If I had, you may depend on it, I'd put up a fight."

"Just as glad you haven't, then," remarked Tony cheerfully.  Carefully, he brought the boat alongside the *Sleuth* and Frank and Joe jumped over the side into their own craft.

Paul Blum was resigned.  He submitted to having his wrists bound with a piece of stout rope that the boys found on the stern of the boat, and then he sat down philosophically.

"I'll get away yet," he told them.  "If I can't escape from that jail myself, my friends will see that I get out."

"How will we get back?" asked Frank, turning to Tony.

Paul Blum laughed.

"That's a problem for you," he said. "The gas tank's empty. What are you going to do about it?"

Tony calmly handed over the can of gasoline from his own boat.

"This should help," he remarked. "I always keep some spare gas on hand."

Paul Blum, beaten, had no more to say. The Hardy boys poured the reserve supply of gasoline into the tank, and in a few minutes the engine was pounding away.

Then, side by side, the two motorboats turned about and put back for Bayport.

# CHAPTER XVI

## A Plan of Action

THE quick work of the Hardy boys and Tony Prito in capturing Paul Blum won them many compliments within the next few days. Even Chief Collig grudgingly admitted that it had been a smart capture. In this he was perhaps largely prompted by a feeling that had Paul Blum made good his escape he, as chief, would have come in for considerable criticism from the townspeople.

As it was, the laxity at the city jail was forgotten in the excitement surrounding the fugitive's return, and Chief Collig was correspondingly relieved. Had Paul Blum not been recaptured, the police force would have had to bear the brunt of public displeasure for having allowed the man to slip through their fingers.

The connection of the Hardy boys with the affair caused many people to recall their previous activities in the Tower Mansion case and the affair of the house on the cliff.

"Those lads will be smart detectives yet,"

more than one person was heard to remark.

Nothing could have pleased the boys more than recognition of the fact that they showed some ability in the profession of their famous father, and, in the light of their recent successes, even Mrs. Hardy was beginning to abandon her prejudices against their desire to be some day more than amateur detectives.

But although Paul Blum was safe in jail, counterfeit money was still being circulated in Bayport and Barmet village.

Hardly a day passed that some one did not report to the police or to the banks that they had been the unwitting victims of the counterfeiters by cashing or accepting spurious bills. In one instance it was a garage owner who had changed a twenty dollar bill for a passing motorist who bought gasoline and oil. In another instance even the steamship ticket office had accepted a false five dollar bill for a ticket and the mistake had not been discovered until the following day. When the ticket, which was bought at a cost of eighty cents, was traced by its number it was found that it had never been presented on the steamboat.

So many instances came to light that the entire city was on guard against the counterfeiters, but so excellent were the imitation bills and so plausible were the excuses of those who sought to pass them on that many people were vicitmized in spite of their caution.

In some cases, merchants were handed counterfeit bills by respectable citizens of Bayport, people who were above reproach, and when the fact was pointed out, the would-be customers explained that they had received the money in good faith from equally reputable citizens. Often the original source of the bad money could not be traced, the counterfeit bills had passed through so many different hands without being discovered.

The boys talked the matter over several times with their father, and one day Fenton Hardy took them into his confidence.

"Don't tell anybody," he said, "but the Federal agents have come across some evidence which makes them think the counterfeiting plant is located somewhere near Barmet village."

"Have they got any definite idea, dad?" asked Joe eagerly.

"They think it is up in the woods—maybe at some farmhouse. You know the country over on the other side of the bay is pretty wild. There would be plenty of hiding places there for counterfeiters."

Mr. Hardy spoke of several places that were being watched, but he admitted that so far the Federal agents had unearthed little of practical value.

They know that most of the bad money is circulated in this vicinity and in and around Boston,'' he concluded. ''It's just possible the plant may be in the Hub.'' There the talk came to an end and the boys walked away as they knew their father was getting ready for a hurried trip to the city.

''It's a good chance for us to do some real detective work,'' said Frank to his brother one afternoon after school, as they were in the gymnasium in the barn back of the Hardy home. ''The whole city is worked up over this counterfeit money business.''

''Smarter detectives than we are are working on the case,'' Joe pointed out, ''but they haven't found much yet.''

''Paul Blum won't talk. If we could get something out of him we might have a clue to go on.''

''He won't say a word. It's my opinion he doesn't know much about the source of the counterfeit money, anyway. I think he was only an agent sent out to dispose of as much of it as he could. They probably have a dozen men traveling around the country passing off these bad bills. Once the money gets into circulation it's liable to pass through a dozen hands before it is discovered.''

''Perhaps that man who stung the garage owner for twenty dollars had no idea the money was bad. And perhaps it's the same way with the fellow who bought the ticket at the steamboat office.''

"It's queer that most of the fuss is being raised right around this city. You don't hear much about it from other places.''

"It's my idea," said Frank, "that the counterfeiters have their plant right in this vicinity.''

"Do you think so?"

"Just as you said—most of the counterfeit money seems to be passed in and around Bayport.''

"Where do you think they could be making the stuff?"

Frank shrugged.

"You never can tell. Perhaps in some cellar of one of the downtown buildings, for all we know. Personally, I've got an idea. It may be foolish, but I've been turning it over in my head for a few days, and the more I think of it, the more reasonable it seems.''

"Spring it.''

"You remember the day we were at the old mill?"

"I'll say I do! Those fellows wouldn't let me dry my clothes in the mill after I'd fished that precious kid out of the water.''

"But one of them offered us a reward, didn't he?"

"Oh, well—you can't take a reward for that."

"That isn't what I'm getting at. Do you remember how the other man grabbed the bills out of his hand and turned his back to us?"

"Sure! He said he wanted to see if they were fives or ones. But it *was* rather funny that he turned his back to us. I thought so at the time. Still, he offered the money to us again."

"But was it the same money?"

Joe was silent. The idea had not occurred to him before.

"Do you mean," he said at last, "that perhaps the fellow changed the bills while he had his back turned?"

"Exactly."

"But why should he do that?"

"Don't you see? Perhaps the first bills were counterfeit. Perhaps the man thought that if we took the counterfeit bills and later found out that they weren't good, we would remember where they came from and start an investigation. This is only a theory, remember; but perhaps the reason he took the bills from the man they called Dock was to change them for good bills, so that we would have no cause for suspicion."

Joe nodded reflectively.

"By gosh, Frank, there may be something to

your idea, after all. Say! Perhaps that's where the counterfeiting plant is. Right in the old mill!''

"That's just what I've been driving at. There's something fishy about the old mill, for all their story that they're making a patent kind of breakfast food. That may be true, of course, but still—"

"They didn't look very much like scientists to me."

"To me, either."

"But how can we find out anything more about the place than we know already? They won't let any one inside the mill, and it's quite evident that they don't want any one around the place at all."

"What made me suspicious," said Frank, "was the fact that Paul Blum seemed to be heading for the mouth of Willow River that afternoon he got away in the motorboat. I began to wonder later if he might have been intending to make his way up as far as the old mill. Perhaps he is connected with the gang."

"It looks reasonable. But if we show our noses around there they'll just chase us away."

"There's Lester."

"Lester?"

"The boy we saved from drowning. We have him on our side anyway, I think. If we haven't, he must be a very ungrateful beggar.

I'd just like to ask him a few questions about this patent breakfast food yarn.''

"That's a good idea!" cried Joe. "If he tells us any kind of story at all we can soon tell if he's lying or not. But, somehow, I don't think he would lie to us. He seemed to me to be a pretty decent sort of boy.''

"That's what I thought of him too. Chances are, if these men are counterfeiters, they're keeping him there as a prisoner. He might be only too glad to tell what he knows, if given a chance.''

"And if it turns out that those men really are scientists and that the mill is really being used for this breakfast food stunt, we won't be making ourselves foolish by poking around and perhaps getting into all sorts of trouble for suspecting they were counterfeiters.''

Frank nodded.

"That was my idea in suggesting Lester. We have to work pretty carefully, for it wouldn't do to start a hue-and-cry and find out that those fellows really are scientists after all. But what do you say to taking the motorcycles to-morrow morning and going up to the old mill to see if we can get to talking to the boy?''

"I'm game. To-morrow's Saturday. Even if the men at the mill do see us they'll think we're just out on a holiday outing. There's no law against going near the old mill, even if they don't want strangers around.''

So the arrangement was made, and the Hardy boys laid their plans for a visit to the old mill on the following day. Each felt that there was something suspicious about the place, some mystery that was not entirely nor satisfactorily solved by the breakfast-food explanation. If they could only talk to Lester, who was already under obligation to them for having saved his life, they felt that they would go a long way toward verifying or dispelling their suspicions regarding the three men who were the present occupants of the mill.

# CHAPTER XVII

## WHAT LESTER SAID

THE Hardy boys set out for the old mill on the following morning.

They went up the shore road by motorcycle, then turned on to the deserted loop that led to the mill on the banks of the Willow River. When they came within sight of the river they left their motorcycles under some trees by the roadside, and went on their way on foot.

They had brought fishing poles and fishing tackle with them.

"We might as well enjoy ourselves while we're on the trip," Frank had said, in making this suggestion. "Besides, it gives us an excuse for being near the mill. There always was good fishing down by the pool near the mill race."

They came out of the woods some distance above the mill and began to fish, working their way slowly down the river. By the time they had come within sight of the mill, Frank had caught two fish and Joe had caught one.

The mill wheel was revolving slowly and they could hear the muffled sound of machinery within the building. Down by the pool they could see a lone figure moving about.

"I believe that's Lester!" exclaimed Joe.

"That's who it is, all right," agreed his brother, after a glance. "And he's fishing, too."

Lester was standing on the bank of the pool, a fishing rod in his hand. But he did not seem to be very enthusiastic about the sport, for there was little eagerness in his expression as he eyed the motionless float on top of the water.

Frank and Joe came slowly down the bank toward him, and he looked up at their approach. He recognized them immediately and a smile came over his face.

"Hello!" he said shyly.

"Hello, Lester," they greeted him. "Any luck?"

"None yet," admitted the lad. "I don't care for fishing, anyway."

"There's supposed to be plenty of fish in this pool," Frank told him.

Lester shrugged his shoulders.

"I suppose so. I've caught quite a few. But when you haven't anything to do but fish all day long you don't care for it so much."

"Is that all you do?" asked Joe.

"That's all. It's mighty lonesome living at this old mill all the time."

"Why don't you go down to the city once in a while?"

"Uncle Dock won't let me."

The boy was evidently lonely and glad to see them. He sat down on the bank and forgot his fishing in his delight at being able to talk to boys of his own age.

"Do you go to school?" he asked wistfully.

The Hardy boys nodded.

"Every day?"

"Every day but Saturdays and Sundays."

"I wish I could go to school. You fellows are lucky."

Joe and Frank looked at one another. This was the first time they had ever met any one who considered that they were fortunate in being able to go to school.

"I suppose we are," admitted Frank, with a smile. "Although sometimes we don't think so."

"Are there lots of other fellows at the school?"

"Quite a few."

Lester sighed.

"Gee, I wish I could go," he said. "But Uncle Dock won't let me go anywhere."

"Where did you come from?" asked Frank.

"Washington. But even there I didn't know

any of the boys. Uncle Dock keeps me with him all the time. But he says we'll be rich some day and then I can have all the friends I want.''

''What does your uncle do for a living?'' inquired Joe.

''Why, he runs the mill,'' answered the boy, evidently surprised by the question.

''But what does he make? Breakfast food?''

''I don't know. I don't know much about it. Uncle Dock never tells me anything.''

''Did he move any new machinery into the mill?'' asked Frank.

''Oh, when we first came here there was a lot of new machinery put in. It's all in a back room.''

''What does it look like?'' Joe inquired lazily.

''I've never seen it. It's in a stone room, and they keep the door locked all the time. Uncle Dock boxed my ears once when he saw me near the door.''

''Have you ever seen any of the breakfast food?''

The boy shook his head.

''I've never seen any yet.''

''Do they ship it all out?''

Lester hesitated.

''Once in a while Mr. Markel goes into the

city with some packages.  But they're never very large.''

"Is Mr. Markel related to you?"

"No.  I never saw the other two men before Uncle Dock brought me here.''

"Is he your real uncle?"

"Oh, yes.  He has looked after me for about a year now, ever since my father died.''

"Is he good to you?" asked Frank.

"Sometimes.  But he won't let me go to school or have any friends, and if I don't do just as he says, he beats me.''

"What did he do when he lived in Washington?" inquired Joe.  "Did he make breakfast food there, too?''

The boy laughed.

"He didn't do very much of anything.  He used to go out at night a lot and leave me all alone.  Sometimes he wouldn't come back until nearly morning.  He told me he was working in a factory.  But sometimes funny looking men would call on him and they'd talk for a long while.''

"And he's never told you anything about the breakfast food?''

"Nothing.''

"How long do you think you'll be here?''

"I don't know.  Uncle Dock says we may be here for a month yet.  But he always has a valise packed so we can go any time.''

The Hardy boys looked at one another significantly.

Was the patent breakfast food enterprise legitimate or illegitimate?

From what the boy had said, there appeared to be grounds for suspicion. It did not seem that Uncle Dock was a scientist after all.

"I wish we were rich now," said Lester. "I'd like to go away from here and go to school. I wish Uncle Dock would move into Bayport so I could go to school with you fellows. But I guess there isn't much chance of that."

"Your uncle is pretty sure he's going to be rich?" said Frank.

"Oh, yes. He has told me often that we'd be rich some day and that I could have all the friends I wanted then."

"He must expect the breakfast food to be a success."

"I suppose so."

"Has he ever bought any grain from the farmers around here?" inquired Joe.

The boy shook his head.

"No. Some people tried to sell grain to him, but he wouldn't buy it."

"Then what is he making the breakfast food out of?"

The boy shrugged his shoulders indifferently.

"I don't know," he answered vaguely. "I don't know much about it. He never tells me anything and he never lets me into the work-room.''

That was the sum and substance of Lester's knowledge of the activities of his Uncle Dock and his two associates. The boy did not seem to object to being questioned; it was plain that he was so lonesome that he welcomed the op-portunity of talking to some one. And the more the Hardy boys interrogated him the more convinced they were that their suspicions of Uncle Dock and the other two men were not unfounded.

''Doesn't he make you do any work?'' asked Frank.

''I have to chop wood once in a while, and bring water up from the spring. But there's not much to do. It's pretty dull here. I wish there was more work for me to do. But mostly I just fish and swim and hang around.''

''Doesn't he let you help him in the mill?''

''No. I've offered to help, but none of them will let me come into the workroom.''

''Workroom? Don't they use the whole mill?''

''Only the stone room where the new ma-chinery is.''

''And the old machinery isn't being used at all?''

''No.''

At that moment there was an interruption. A shout from the mill attracted their attention and, looking up, they saw Uncle Dock standing in the doorway.

"Lester!" be bellowed angrily.

"Yes?"

"Come up here this minute," ordered the old man. He left the door and came down the slope toward the river.

"Now I'm in for it," said the boy. "I suppose he'll be angry now because I was talking to you."

Uncle Dock was indeed angry. As he came up to the group he was muttering beneath his breath.

"Get back up to the mill, you young rascal!" he ordered, giving Lester a cuff on the side of the head. "How often have I told you not to be talking to strangers. You talk too much altogether. Get back up to the mill and stay there."

"We were just chatting—" began the boy, but Uncle Dock silenced him with a blow.

With an appealing glance at the Hardy boys, Lester began to make his way back up the slope toward the mill. Uncle Dock turned toward Joe and Frank, surveying them resentfully.

"What are you doing, loafing around here?" he demanded.

"We're not loafing. We have been fishing in the river," said Frank. "Not that it's any of your business, so far as I can see."

"I'll marke it my business," thundered Uncle Dock. "You two fellows had better stay away from here after this. We don't want you hanging around here."

"The river is free," Joe reminded him.

"Keep away from around this mill or I'll make it hot for you. What was that rascal of a boy telling you?"

"We were just talking," replied Frank evasively.

"Well, don't talk to him again. I don't want him mixing up with all the riff-raff of the country and talking to every Tom, Dick and Harry that comes around. I'll thank you to stay away from here after this."

Whereupon Uncle Dock, still grumbling indignantly, went stamping up the slope again toward the mill. The Hardy boys, not a bit alarmed by the outburst, but feeling that they had gained valuable information that day, began to move slowly down the river bank away from the vicinity of the old mill.

# CHAPTER XVIII

## SUSPICIONS

"WHAT do you think, Joe?" asked Frank, as they were speeding back to Bayport on their motorcycles.

"I don't think Uncle Dock is a scientist any more than I am."

"That's my opinion, too. Why should they have so much secrecy about a new kind of breakfast food? Why won't they even let Lester into the workroom with them?"

"Something fishy about it. And it's plain by now that Uncle Dock doesn't like strangers around the place."

"That poor kid must lead a lonely life with that gang. It's a wonder he doesn't run away from them."

"He has no place else to go, I suppose. He seems a nice sort of chap, too," Joe answered.

"Well, we didn't get anything definite from him, but we know enough to make us mighty suspicious of what's going on in that old mill."

144

"I'd just like to get a look at that machinery in the secret room the boy mentioned."

Frank was silent for a while.

"I wish Uncle Dock hadn't seen us there to-day. It'll make it awkward now if we ever go back. He has told us to stay away, and now he'll be suspicious if he ever sees us around there again."

"We might tell dad what we know about the place."

But Frank vetoed this suggestion.

"I'd rather work along our own lines until we get something more definite," he said. "If we get some real evidence we can tell dad about it. So far we have nothing to go on but our own suspicions."

All the way back to Bayport, the Hardy boys discussed the various aspects of the case, and although they agreed that the mysterious activities of the three men at the old mill tended to indicate almost anything but scientific endeavors, they realized that if they investigated too thoroughly they might get into serious trouble.

"We'll just wait a while and keep our ears open," Frank decided. "If those fellows are in the counterfeiting game they'll do something to give themselves away. And then we'll be right on the job."

When the boys arrived home they amused

themselves in the gymnasium in the barn for some time, had an impromptu boxing match and finally, after a shower bath, went down street. It was a sleepy Saturday afternoon and the city was very quiet.

"Nothing much doing around here," remarked Frank. "We should have stayed out in the country."

"We could go out in the motorboat for a while."

"Fine. Let's go."

But at that moment they heard the whistle of the afternoon express. Like most boys, they had a weakness for trains. There was a fascination about the great locomotives that held them spellbound and they liked nothing better than to watch the trains that passed through Bayport and to speculate on the towns and cities they had come from or were bound for. At times when school became exceptionally distasteful they had often gone down to the railway station and wished they could board the first train that came by, to travel on to strange countries. Somehow, they had never been so daring as to do this, common sense invariably coming to the rescue, but the lure of locomotives and shining rails still held them in its grasp.

They moved down the street toward the station and came out on the platform just as the

express was pulling in. Idly, they watched the
few passengers who emerged from the coaches,
envied the engineer who was lolling majesti-
cally in the cab, watched the conductor in his
smart uniform, and looked at the people who
were boarding the train.

Suddenly Frank nudged his brother.

"Isn't that Markel?" he asked.

Joe followed his glance. Near the steps of
one of the Pullman coaches was a familiar figure, with cap pulled down over his eyes. There
was no mistaking the fellow; he was indeed
Markel, one of the associates of Uncle Dock at
the old mill.

What particularly attracted the boys' attention, however, was the fact that Markel carried
a bulky paper package under his arm.

He had not seen them, but there was something so furtive in his manner that the Hardy
boys made themselves as inconspicuous as possible in the shadow of one of the pillars near
by.

Markel lounged about near the coach, now
and then glancing up anxiously, as though expecting some one.

Within a few minutes, just as the conductor
shouted, "All aboard!" a tall, thin-faced man
with a neat black mustache, emerged from the
coach. He glanced hastily down at Markel,
nodded swiftly, said something in a low tone,

and Markel forthwith handed him the package. The tall man snatched it from his grasp, turned and retreated quickly into the coach again.

Markel, as soon as this transaction had been completed gave a shrug of his shoulders as though he had been relieved of an unpleasant burden, turned swiftly on his heel and walked away. He disappeared into the station just as the train began to pull out.

The whole affair had occupied but a few seconds and had passed almost unnoticed by any one on the platform save the Hardy boys. Any who may have noticed the handing over of the package doubtless attached little importance to it. The Hardy boys themselves would not have given it more than a passing glance had it not been for Markel's connection with the mystery of the old mill.

"What do you make of that, Frank?"

"Markel must have passed on a sample of the new breakfast food."

"He seemed mighty secretive about it."

"I'll say he did. You'd think it was a bomb he was handing over instead of breakfast food. He waited until the train was just pulling out before the other man came for it."

"No breakfast food about that performance."

"I don't think so either. Evidently Markel and the gang are in touch with some one in the city. You remember that Lester said Markel came into Bayport every little while with a package under his arm. That must have been one of them.''

''Well, that's a little more evidence to go on.''

''Give them enough rope and they'll hang themselves. I'll just bet dollars to doughnuts that there is counterfeit money in that package instead of breakfast food. This man Markel looks to me like a crook, and his tall friend on the train didn't look any too trustworthy either. My idea is that they are using the mill as a plant where they turn out the money, then they give it to one of their men on the train and he takes it to some other city for distribution.''

''That looks like it,'' Joe agreed. ''You could tell that Markel had something on his conscience when he handed that package over. He looked mighty shifty about it.''

The boys walked back down the street, still discussing the events of the day. They spent the rest of the afternoon out in Barmet Bay, in the *Sleuth*. For the time being, they dismissed the affair of the mill from their minds, being content, as Frank had said, that the counterfeiters, if they were such, would ultimately betray themselves.

When they returned home that evening for supper they did not tell their father what they had learned. But Fenton Hardy himself brought up the question of counterfeit money when he told them that he had that afternoon received a telegram from Federal authorities asking him to further his investigations.

They have evidence that more than ten thousand dollars in counterfeit money was put into circulation within the past three days,'' he told the boys. "The affair is going beyond all bounds.''

"And Paul Blum is still silent?'' asked Frank.

"Can't get a word out of him. I'm inclined to believe he doesn't know anything about the men who are at the head of the organization. I think he was only a tool, employed to get the money in circulation. But I wish you two lads would keep on the lookout for any clues. It will help me a lot if we can run these counter-feiters to earth. Then, besides, there is a big reward.''

"We'll do our best,'' they promised.

And, secretly, they wondered what Fenton Hardy would think if he knew how much work they had already put on the case and how much evidence they had already gathered, tending to indicate that the old mill on the Willow River was in some way connected with the ac-tivities of the counterfeiting gang.

"If you can get anything definite in this

case," said Fenton Hardy, with a smile, "I'll be ready to admit that you have some abilities as detectives—"

"Fenton, don't encourage them," objected Mrs. Hardy.

"Nonsense, Laura," he replied. "If they want to be detectives and if they have the talent for it, you might as well try to keep water from running downhill as to stop them. They've done good work on two difficult cases already."

"And I have a hunch that we'll do something on this case, too," said Frank, with confidence.

# CHAPTER XIX

## THE RUG BUYER

Two days later an event occurred that brought the activities of the counterfeiters much closer home.

Frank and Joe returned from school on Monday afternoon to find their mother in a state of great agitation. The moment they entered the house they could tell that something unusual had happened, for Mrs. Hardy was sitting by the living-room table gazing disconsolately at a great heap of bills in her lap.

"Where'd you get all the money, mother?" asked Frank, jokingly at first. But his expression became serious when he saw the anxiety and distress in Mrs. Hardy's face. Her fingers were trembling as she picked up the bills and put them on the table.

"What's the matter?" asked Joe quickly. "What's wrong?"

Mrs. Hardy got up and walked across the room toward the window. She looked out at the street for a while, then turned to her sons.

"You didn't see a foreign rug buyer around the streets this afternoon, did you?" she asked them.

The Hardy boys shook their heads.

"Just came from school," they told her. "We didn't meet anybody on the way." Suddenly Frank glanced at the floor. "Why, you've sold the rug!" he exclaimed, in surprise.

The living-room floor had hitherto been covered by a valuable old Persian rug, as soft as moss. It had been bought by Mr. Hardy when on a trip to the city, but Mrs. Hardy had never cared for it. Fenton Hardy had thought to surprise his wife when he brought the rug home, but in a masculine indifference to color schemes he had neglected to see to it that the rug matched the rest of the room. Its color was not what Mrs. Hardy wanted, and inasmuch as the rug had been purchased at an exclusive sale, they had found it impossible to exchange it at the time.

Mrs. Hardy had always said that if she had an opportunity she would get rid of the rug and purchase something different. However, the opportunity was long in coming. Although she had received several offers for it, none of these had been for more than five hundred dollars.

"And," as she said, "I refuse to sell a nine hundred dollar rug for that price."

Now, as the Hardy boys noticed, the rug was gone.

"How much did you get for it?" asked Joe eagerly.

"I gave it away."

"Gave it away?" they exclaimed.

Mrs. Hardy nodded.

"Not intentionally. I've been cheated."

"How?" demanded Frank quickly.

Mrs. Hardy motioned toward the money.

"I've just been to the bank to deposit that money—"

"You don't mean to say it's counterfeit?"

"So the bank cashier told me."

Frank sat down heavily in the nearest chair.

"Well I'll be gosh-hanged!" he exclaimed. "How did this happen? How much did they sting you for?"

"Eight hundred dollars," answered Mrs. Hardy gravely.

Joe whistled in surprise.

"How did it happen?"

"He came here shortly after you boys left for school," began Mrs. Hardy. "It must have been a little before two o'clock."

"Who came here?"

"The rug buyer. He was a queer little fellow, very short and dark. He was a foreigner, you could tell by his appearance. He didn't speak very good English. He was dark and swarthy, with little, keen black eyes.  He came up to the front door and asked me if I wanted to buy rugs.  When I told him that I didn't want to buy he asked if I had any to sell.  He said he was a traveling rug merchant and that he went from city to city, buying and selling and trading rugs."

"So you told him about the living-room rug?" suggested Frank.

"I just thought of it then, and I thought it might be a good chance to get rid of it and perhaps get a better rug in its stead.  I mentioned that I had a rug that I might sell, but I told him I didn't think he could pay the price."

"And he asked to see it anyway?" Frank went on.

"When I told him I didn't think he could buy it he merely laughed in a very shrewd sort of way and said that money was no object to him, that he had bought rugs costing as much as two thousand dollars and turned them over at a profit.  So I asked him to come into the house and the moment he saw the rug he admired it very much.  He asked me how much I wanted for it, so I told him I wanted nine hundred dollars.  Of course, I didn't expect to get that much, because that is all the rug cost, but these fellows always haggle over price, so it's best to name a good stiff figure right at the start."

The Hardy boys smiled at this evidence of their mother's shrewdness.

"He said he wouldn't give me nine hundred dollars but he offered seven hundred dollars. I told him that his price was ridiculous, but asked if he had any rugs he wanted to trade for it. He looked rather dubious when I mentioned a trade, and said that while he carried some medium priced rugs with him he carried nothing that could equal the one I wished to sell."

"Did he say where he kept these other rugs?" Frank asked.

"He said they were at his hotel but that his more valuable rugs were all in the city and that it would take a day or so before he could have them sent here. However, he said that he would buy the rug from me for eight hundred dollars and take a chance on being able to sell me a good rug when he should have them sent down from the city."

"Fair enough," remarked Joe.

"It seemed fair enough to me, for of course the rug was worth only about eight hundred dollars, perhaps less, because it has been used for several months. I was under no obligation to buy a new rug from him unless I wished, so I accepted his offer and he paid me the money."

"Eight hundred dollars!"

"In cash. He seemed to carry a great deal

of money in a heavy leather wallet. He gave me the money in fifties and fives, and I thought very well of myself for making such a good bargain."

"Until you came to bank the money," Frank said.

"Until I came to bank the money. The cashier glanced at the bills, then told me he was sorry, but that he couldn't accept them. For a moment I didn't understand him, because I had forgotten all about this scare about counterfeit money and hadn't given the matter a thought. Then he told me that the bills were counterfeit. So there was nothing left for me to do but come back home, realizing that I had been very neatly tricked."

"But perhaps you haven't been tricked after all," suggested Frank. "It may be possible that the rug buyer didn't realize the money was bad. Did he say what hotel he was staying at?"

"Yes, he told me, but I called up the police and asked them to find him for me. They investigated and found that there had been no rug buyer staying at that hotel all week, nor at any other hotel in Bayport, so far as they could find."

"That doesn't look so good."

"What's more, they made inquiries at the station and found that a man answering to his description had taken the early afternoon train out. He took the rug with him—not only my rug, but a rug that he had bought from another woman in Bayport.''

''He'll probably sell them in some other town.''

''Just what he did. They found that he had bought a ticket to the next city but when they got in touch with the police there they found that he had sold the two rugs to a wholesale firm and disappeared. He sold my rug for five hundred dollars, and the other one for three hundred dollars.''

''Did he give the other woman counterfeit money, too?''

''Yes.''

''He cleaned up on that afternoon's work,'' remarked Frank. ''He didn't lose any time in getting away, either.''

''If I had only gone to the bank early it might have been different,'' said Mrs. Hardy. ''As it was, I got there only a few minutes before three o'clock, and by the time I got in touch with the police and by the time they had tried to trace the man here and later found where he had gone—you know how slow they are—it was too late.''

''I guess there's no chance of seeing him back in two days with the rug he wanted to sell you,'' observed Frank. ''Either he is in

league with the counterfeiters or else he was
stung himself for a lot of counterfeit money
and decided to get rid of it as smoothly as possible.''

Mrs. Hardy was downcast.

"I should have been on my guard," she said.
"There has been so much of this bad money
going around that I should have been on watch
for it, especially with a big sum like eight hundred dollars. It's my own fault, I suppose,
but it's hard to lose that much money." She
glanced at the heap of bills on the table. "It's
not worth the paper it's printed on."

Frank picked up one of the bills and examined it.

"Looks just like the five that the fellow
passed on to Joe and me at the station," he
commented, testing the quality of the paper.
"It comes from the same source, I'll bet."

"Eight hundred dollars!" Joe exclaimed.
"That's the biggest haul yet. I'd like to have
that rug merchant by the back of the neck
right this minute. I'd shake the eight hundred out of him in a hurry."

"I guess there's not much chance of catching him now. He has sold the rugs and made
his getaway."

Mrs. Hardy was silent. She felt the loss of
the valuable rug very keenly, and still more
keenly did she feel the ignominy of having been

imposed upon after all the warnings that **had** been circulated regarding counterfeit money. But the rug merchant had been so plausible, and as she was an unsuspecting woman by nature, she had never for a moment considered the possibility of trickery.

"We'll go down and have a chat with the police," said Frank, getting up. "Although I'm afraid it won't do any good."

"Chief Collig will tell us that he is busy following up clues," remarked Joe, with a laugh. "And that's as far as he'll ever get."

This proved to be the case. When the boys reached the police station they found Chief Collig and Detective Smuff in the midst of a game of pinochle and averse to being disturbed.

When they inquired if there had been any further information regarding the rug merchant, Chief Collig shook his head.

"We're following up some clues," he said gravely; "but there hasn't been any more trace of him."

"Not a trace," corroborated Detective Smuff, with a portentous frown.

"Do you think he'll be arrested?" asked Frank.

Chief Collig looked up.

"Of course he'll be arrested," he declared. "Didn't I say we're followin' up clues? We'll have the fellow behind the bars all right."

"I'm workin' on the case myself," said Detective Smuff, examining his cards wearily.

"Rely on us," advised the chief. "Your play, Smuff."

The boys retired. Somehow, they got the impression that the Bayport police department was not exerting a great deal of effort to try to capture the fraudulent rug buyer.

# CHAPTER XX

## A Note of Warning

THREE days later, Fenton Hardy, who had been away from home on business, received a note.

No one saw the man who left it at the door. The Hardy boys were at school and Mrs. Hardy was busy in the kitchen. She heard the front doorbell ring and went to answer it.

But when she opened the door there was no one in sight.

She looked out and saw a man walking briskly down the opposite side of the street. A woman with a baby-carriage was strolling past the house, and farther down the street two men were standing talking on the corner.

Somewhat surprised, and imagining that her ears must have deceived her, she was about to close the door when she became aware of a white object that had fluttered to her feet.

It was a cheap envelope, sealed, and with the name of Fenton Hardy written on it in pencil.

Mrs. Hardy picked it up, examined it curi-

ously, then brought it into the house and placed
it on the table in her husband's study. It was
not an unusual occurrence to have letters left
at the door in this manner, as occasionally
anonymous letters were left for the detective,
giving him hints or advice concerning cases on
which he was engaged. To most of these he
paid no attention, although sometimes valuable
information was brought to his notice in this
manner.

This, Mrs. Hardy judged, was another such
communication, which was why the person who
delivered it had been careful to hurry away
after ringing the bell.

Mr. Hardy did not return home until late
that afternoon. He had been over to Barmet
village where the Federal authorities were
closely watching two men thought to be in
league with the counterfeiters. Mr. Hardy had
followed one man to a near-by city and seen the
fellow pass a small package to a woman in
black, who had quickly disappeared in a crowd.
But the noted detective knew the woman and
knew where she could be located when wanted.

The boys had arrived back from school, had
left their books at the house, and had set out
with Chet Morton for a cruise in the motorboat. When Mr. Hardy came back he glanced
over his mail and was settling down to read the
evening paper when his wife remembered the

note that had been left at the door that afternoon.

"Some one left a letter for you this afternoon," she said. "I heard the doorbell ring,
but when I went to answer it there was no one
at the door. I picked up a letter, though, and
I put it on your study table."

Fenton Hardy went into the study and
picked up the letter, slitting open the envelope.
Within, was a thin sheet of cheap paper on
which had been written a few lines in pencil.

He read the message with a slow smile, then
handed the paper over to his wife.

"Some one trying to scare me," he said.

She picked up the note. In a crude, ill-
formed hand, she read the following:

*"Better give up this counterfeit case or
we'll take the shirt off your back. We
know this game too well. Let this be a
warning to you. Poor Blum is a rank out-
sider. Better let him go."*

Mrs. Hardy looked up anxiously.

"What are you going to do about this note?"
she asked.

The detective shrugged.

"Ignore it, of course."

"But they may harm you."

"They may try. They won't be the first

ones who have tried to frighten me away from a case.''

''But they must be right in Bayport, to deliver a note like this.''

''I've suspected all along that their headquarters were here. Don't worry, Laura. I'm not afraid of them.''

''But I *do* worry. They're desperate men. They'll stop at nothing.''

Fenton Hardy laughed.

''It isn't the first time I've been threatened. It's only a bluff. I'll stay right on the case— although so far I haven't been able to make much progress on it.

''But this matter of the note is adding insult to injury, don't you think? First of all they send one of their men around here to fool us to the extent of eight hundred dollars with their counterfeit money, and now they try to frighten me away from handling the case any further.''

Fenton Hardy looked at the note again, then replaced it carefully in the envelope.

''You didn't see any one on the street after the doorbell rang?'' he asked.

''Oh, there were three or four people walking by, but I didn't notice any of them particularly. They all seemed quite average people. None of them looked at all suspicious.''

"The chap that delivered the note was prob ably hiding around the corner of the house until you went inside again. That's their usual scheme. It wouldn't have done much good if you had seen him. Probably some chap they picked up on the street and bribed to slip the note into the door."

"I don't like it!"

At that moment Frank and Joe came into the house, flushed from their outing on the bay. They were laughing at the recollection of some remarkable acrobatic feats that Chet Morton had attempted on the bow of the motorboat, the result of which had been the sudden immersion of Chet in the chilly waters of the bay. He had just left them, his clothes dripping wet, heading for home on his motorcycle, vowing that he could have stood on his hands on the bow of the boat if only Frank hadn't steered to the left when he should have steered to the right.

"However," he had said cheerfully, "I missed my bath last Saturday night, anyway, so this will make up for it."

The Hardy boys recounted their adventures and after Fenton Hardy had chuckled over the plight of Chet he tossed over the mysterious letter to them.

"What do you think of that?" he asked of the boys.

Frank and Joe read the scrawled warning with interest.

"Trying to frighten you away from the case, are they?" said Frank, as he gave back the note.

"Looks like it."

"You won't pay any attention to it, of course?"

"Not a bit. Although your mother seems to think I'll be carried home on a stretcher any day."

"When did the note come?" Joe inquired with deep interest.

Mrs. Hardy told them how the strange letter had been delivered, and when they learned that it had been left at the door instead of being sent through the post-office both boys became immediately excited. They did not, however, air their suspicions at the time and it was not until they were alone after supper that they discussed the topic between them.

"That settles it!" declared Frank with finality. "The counterfeiters *must* be right here in Bayport."

"Or near by."

"That's what I mean. If they were out of town, the letter would have been sent by mail."

"It's getting to be a little too much. As dad said, it was adding insult to injury—tricking mother to the extent of eight hundred dollars and now sending an impudent note like that. It's up to us to use what we know."

"You mean to see if we can find out anything more about the mill?"

"I mean to find out everything there is to be found out about it."

"I'm with you. When do we start?"

"When should we?"

"To-night."

"So soon?"

"Why not?"

"It's all right with me."

"If we're going to go back there at all we may as well get it over with as soon as we can," said Frank. "I've been thinking over a way to get away with it and I think we should be able to get inside that place and investigate it without much trouble."

"How?"

"Do you remember how Carl Stummer remarked that you looked something like Lester?"

"Yes."

"And there *is* a bit of a resemblance, too. You are of about the same build, and you both have fair, curly hair. I think you should be able to impersonate him if we went around there at night. At a distance, and at night time, they might mistake you for him, even if we were discovered."

"I never thought of that," Joe admitted. "It isn't a bad idea. I'm willing to try it."

"It will be risky, of course. But I'm practically convinced that the old mill is where this counterfeit money is coming from. The only way we'll ever find out is to go there ourselves. If we told the town police what we suspected they would only laugh at us and probably they'd be so clumsy about taking any action that the counterfeiters would get wind of it. The only way is to keep it to ourselves and go out there quietly and see what we can find."

"How can we get out to-night? Mother won't let us go. She'll be afraid we'll get hurt."

"I hate to do anything underhand, but it's our only chance. We'll go out for a motorcycle trip this evening, and as soon as it gets dark we'll head for the mill. We should reach there about ten o'clock. We'll park the bikes a good distance away from the mill, so they won't hear us coming, and then we'll walk the rest of the way."

"If we get the goods on the counterfeiters we'll be heroes. If we don't we'll catch a lecture for staying out late."

"We'll just have to take our chance on that. But I think that if everything goes well we won't get any lecture."

"How'll we get into the mill?" asked Joe.

"We'll have to wait until we get there be-fore we lay our plans. I've sort of forgotten the layout of the place. But if we work it right I think we should be able to get inside. I'd like to get into that mysterious stone room that Lester mentioned, and see what sort of machinery they have in there. I'll bet it's an engraving plant and a printing press instead of a patent breakfast food machine."

"What if we're caught—"

"That's a chance we're taking. We've got to risk it. What if we find that the place is really the headquarters of this counterfeit gang? Look at it that way."

So for the rest of the evening the boys were conspicuously studious. They were occupied with their books until twilight fell, after which Frank yawned and murmured that he would like a breath of fresh air.

"Think I'll go out for a little spin on the motorcycle," he said casually.

"I'll go with you," observed Joe promptly.

Fenton Hardy looked up.

"Yes, you've been in the house all evening. Go ahead."

"Don't be long," advised Mrs. Hardy.

"We won't be any longer than we can help," said Frank mysteriously.

With that, the Hardy boys left the house

and went out to the garage for their motor-cycles.

They drove around the streets of Bayport for some time until at last it grew darker. Then they headed their machines out toward the shore road. The moon was just rising over the bay when they left the city, and they drove at good speed into the country.

"Now to tackle the old mill!" exclaimed Frank.

# CHAPTER XXI

## AT THE MILL

THE two boys made good time out into the country and when at last they reached the abandoned road that led down to Willow River it was not quite ten o'clock. As they rode they discussed their plan of action and it was agreed that they should leave the motorcyles beside the road at the same place they had left them on the occasion of their previous visit to the mill.

"I'd like to have them closer to the river," said Frank, "for we might have to clear out of there in a hurry. But we can't afford to let them hear us coming."

"And it's a calm night. They could hear a motorcycle for half a mile," opined his brother.

They left the machines in the shade of some trees by the roadside and went the rest of the way on foot. They could see quite clearly, for the moon had risen higher and the grey ribbon of road extended before them.

"I wish it had been a bit darker," Joe said. "We'll have to be careful when we get near the place."

"They may have some one posted on guard. Oh, well, we can look the place over when we get there."

At last they emerged on the hilltop that overlooked Willow River.

Below them lay the stream, with water shining in the moonlight. The deep banks of willow trees along the borders cast heavy shadows, and a light mist overhung the fields and hedges in the distance.

Gloomy and mysterious, the heavy bulk of the old mill rose from beside the river, near the shimmering silver streak of the mill race. Not a light shone from the building and it appeared absolutely deserted.

"Perhaps they've all moved away," suggested Joe.

"I noticed that the buildings were all boarded up when we were here last time. They haven't moved away, never fear."

Cautiously, the boys went down the slope.

They left the road and kept to the shadows of the trees, skirting the open space of meadow that lay between the grove and the mill itself. They did not speak, for the night was so calm and clear that sound carried for a considerable distance. They could hear the dull roar of the rapids and the waterfall, sounding hollow and lonely in the moonlit night.

They came to the edge of the grove and moved slowly about in the deep shadows, the grass sinking beneath their feet. When they had reached a point about two hundred feet from the mill they paused to reconnoitre.

"We've got to cross that open space," whispered Frank.

"And what then?"

"See that willow tree beside the mill?"

Joe nodded.

"It reaches right to the roof. It looks to be our best bet. If we can climb that tree and drop to the roof o.` get in a window we'll be all right."

"As long as we can get up the tree without being heard."

"We have to take our chances on that," Frank said, in a low voice. "I think it's going to be harder to cross that open space."

For two hundred feet the grassy sward was bathed in moonlight. They could not walk across it without being in full view of any one who might be watching from the mill. But it had to be crossed as the mill itself was isolated on the bank of the river and on this side there was no protecting shade to enable them to creep up closer.

"We'll have to crawl across the grass," Frank whispered. "Ready?"

"I'm ready."

"Go easy and quiet. If you hear a sound, don't move."

They dropped to their hands and knees, then left the shadow of the wood. They began to crawl slowly toward the willow tree at the rear of the mill.

Inch by inch they made their way forward.

The moon was high in the sky and seemed like a giant searchlight. It seemed impossible that they could cross that open space without being discovered. Every blade of grass seemed clearly revealed by the moonlight.

When they were about half way toward the mill they heard a sound in the distance.

It was the banging of a heavy door.

There was a warning whisper from Frank. They lay motionless in the thick grass.

For a moment a deep silence prevailed. Then, from the mill, they heard a surly voice:

"I saw some one out on the hillside."

They were startled. But still they did not move. Their only hope of safety lay in silence and in remaining motionless.

"You're crazy, Markel," replied some one. "There's no one out there."

"I tell you I saw some one crawling down through the grass. I'm sure of it. I saw him from that upper window."

"Whereabouts?"

"Out there—see? Can't you see something dark up there?"

There was silence for a moment or so. Then the second man laughed.

"It's only a log."

"I tell you, it isn't a log. A log doesn't move."

"That isn't moving."

"It was."

"Well, if you're so sure of it, why don't you go on up and see? You're getting so nervous lately that you think people are hanging around here all the time."

"I've got a right to be nervous. We're not safe here, I tell you. We should have moved out of here a week ago."

"We'll never find a place as safe as this."

"Is that so? Ever since those two boys came snooping around here and asking Lester questions I've been suspicious. They've got their eye on this place, let me tell you. They were down at the railway station the day I slipped the package to Burgess, and I'm mighty sure they saw me."

"Just a couple of kids. You're too nervous."

"Well, I'm going up on the hill and take a look at that log, as you call it."

As it happened, there was a log lying in the grass close by Frank. But he realized that if Markel came up to investigate he would have no chance to evade discovery. They could not get up and run away—at least not until capture seemed inevitable. Frank's heart sank. They had been discovered before they had a chance even to reach the mill.

At that moment relief came from a most unexpected quarter.

A dark cloud that had been creeping across the sky began to obscure the moon, and gradually the vivid illumination that bathed the hillside gave way to gloom and darkness. The cloud hid the moon completely.

"Now's our chance!" whispered Frank, to his brother. "Head toward the willow tree."

He scrambled to his feet and together the boys raced down the slope toward the willow tree back of the mill. Their feet made no sound in the deep grass. They were taking a desperate chance, they knew, for, in spite of the cloud that had fallen across the moon, Markel might be able to see them.

But Markel had just emerged from the mill and his eyes were not yet accustomed to the gloom. As the boys reached the shelter of the willow tree, the moon emerged from behind the cloud and slowly the hillside was again bathed in radiance.

Panting, the boys halted beneath the tree and looked back.

They could see the dark figure of Markel as he cut across the slope in a diagonal direction and they watched as he drew near the place where they had been lying.

They saw him stop, kick at something in the grass, then they heard him mutter as he turned away.

"Well, what was it?" called the other man from the doorway of the mill.

"It was a log all right," admitted Markel in a disgruntled tone. "But I could have sworn I saw it move a while ago."

"Better get your eyes tested."

To this pleasantry Markel made no reply, but trudged on down the slope until he again reached the mill. The boys pressed close to the willow tree.

"You may think I'm being too careful," they heard Markel saying. "But we've got good reason to be careful. You know what'll happen to the whole crowd of us if we're caught."

"Sure. About twenty years in the pen. But we're not going to be caught I tell you."

"Don't be too sure. We can't afford to take chances, anyway. I'd rather keep my eyes open and get fooled by a few logs on the hill-

side than feel too safe and spend the rest of
my life behind the bars."

"I guess you're right. Anyway, everything
is all right to-night."

"I'm going to take a trip around the mill,
anyhow."

"Your nerves must be jumpy."

"They are," snapped Markel. "My nerves
are always jumpy when I think I see something
moving down toward here from the woods—
and I don't care whether that was a log or not,
I saw something move."

"Oh, probably a sheep or a cow that strayed
from one of the farms. Or even a dog."

"Yes, it might have been a dog," Markel admitted.

"We'd better get to work. Dock is waiting
for us."

"I'm going to walk around the mill once,
anyway."

"Go ahead. Go ahead, then," said the other
man. "I'll be inside with Dock."

The boys heard heavy footsteps as Markel
left the doorway, and then they saw his dark
figure in the moonlight as he came around the
side of the mill.

They pressed close against the willow tree
and lowered their heads so that their faces
would not be seen. Both were wearing dark
clothes and dark caps. They did not look up,

for they knew that their faces would be grey against the surrounding darkness and that Markel might see them.

In an agony of suspense they heard the footsteps come closer.

Markel poked around among the rubbish at the side of the mill. It was plain that he was not yet convinced that he had been suffering from a delusion when he saw the moving forms on the hillside and he meant to satisfy himself beyond any shadow of doubt that there was no one lurking in the vicinity of the mill.

Nearer and nearer he came.

His body brushed against the overhanging branches of the willow. He was now only a few yards away from the Hardy boys.

Breathlessly, they waited. They stood, rigid and motionless, not daring to look up.

Markel's footsteps came to a stop. He was standing but a short distance away, listening intently.

Had he seen them?

# CHAPTER XXII

## Through the Roof

THE Hardy boys always said that the few seconds in which they stood in the shadow of the willow tree with the suspicious Markel almost within arm's length of them, not knowing whether they had been discovered or not, were the longest seconds they had ever known.

It seemed hours before they finally heard Markel give a grunt of satisfaction and trudge away in the opposite direction.

Even then it was minutes before they dared move, before they ventured to raise their heads and look about them. When at last they did so, Markel was no longer in sight.

They heard him go around the other side of the mill and finally they heard his footsteps as he trudged up into the doorway.

The door banged at last.

Markel was back in the mill. They breathed freely.

"That was a close call," whispered Joe, in relief.

"Not a sound," cautioned Frank. "They may be listening."

They waited in the shadows for a long time. But evidently Markel had given up the search, his suspicions allayed. Finally a strange sound came from the interior of the mill, a strange whirring sound, followed by the muffled rumble of machinery.

"What's that?" whispered Joe.

They listened. The rumbling sound rose and fell with monotonous regularity. Finally Frank nudged his brother and pointed to one of the boarded windows half way up the side of the mill.

A faint streak of light was apparent through a crack in the boards.

"That must be where their workroom is," Frank whispered.

The sound of machinery in motion continued.

"We've struck them at the right time," said Joe, in a low voice. "They must do their work at night."

"We've got to make sure."

"How can we get inside the mill?"

"The willow tree. We'll have to climb it and drop down on the roof."

"What if they hear us? We won't have a chance to get away."

"They won't hear us," said Frank confidently. "The walls are of stone. Anyway, the sound of machinery will drown out any noises from outside. It's our only chance to get into the mill."

"Lead the way, then."

Frank began to ascend the willow tree.

It was difficult work, for although the tree was large, it bent and swayed under his weight. It was impossible for both of them to attempt to climb at the same time, and Joe was forced to wait on guard at the bottom, listening as his brother made his way higher and higher among the springy branches.

The topmost branches drooped over the roof of the mill, and when at length Frank had reached them he swung himself over until his feet touched the top of the building. For a second or so he was uncertain of his footing but at length he was able to stand steadily on the sloping surface. He released his grasp and the branches swished back. So far he had been able to move with a minimum of noise and he was confident that his ascent to the roof had been unheard.

He called softly to Joe, and in a few minutes a rustling among the branches indicated that his brother was also climbing the tree.

Frank waited and directed his brother so that Joe was soon swinging out from the branches. He dropped lightly to the roof of the old mill.

"There should be some sort of trapdoor here," said Frank quietly. "If there isn't we'll have to lower ourselves over the edge to one of the upper windows. I noticed a small open window around at the front. But there is probably a trapdoor."

The mill roof was not on an abrupt slant, so that the boys were able to make their way along among the shingles without a great deal of difficulty. The roof was in a bad state of repair, and once Frank came upon a wide hole, where the shingles had fallen off and where the wood beneath had rotted away.

But there was no trapdoor.

"We'll tackle that hole in the roof," he decided.

The gap was only about a foot square, but when Frank turned his flashlight on it he saw that immediately beneath them was a sort of attic, the topmost room in the mill.

Quietly, they began enlarging the hole in the roof. Fortunately, the effect of rain and wind and weather had been such as to render the roof extremely weak. The singles broke off easily, and bit by bit they made the hole wider until at last it was a large, black gap.

They did not throw the débris to the ground, but piled it carefully up on the roof near by. The work of enlarging the hole in the roof had taken them some time, as they worked cautiously and deliberately with a view to a minimum of noise. Finally they agreed that there was sufficient space to admit the passage of a human body, and Frank began to lower himself through the opening.

The attic was very low, only about five feet from floor to roof, and when Frank's feet touched the boards beneath he tested their strength. Having satisfied himself that the floor was strong enough to support his weight, he crouched down, flashing the light about him in search of some mode of egress to the lower part of the building.

He cautioned Joe to wait on the roof. The condition of the building was such that the floor might not be strong enough to hold them both, in which event disaster would overtake them.

At first he thought the attic was entirely separated from the rest of the mill. The floor seemed to be solid. There was not the sign of a stairway or opening of any kind.

Frank was bitterly disappointed. To have been successful so far and then find themselves in a narrow little room under the eaves of the mill!

Suddenly he caught sight of a crack between the boards, and he held the flashlight closer to investigate. He found a space about two feet square, evidently a trapdoor cut in the floor, and he tugged at the edges of this until at length he managed to raise one side of it. Then, quietly, he worked at the trapdoor until he was able to lift it out of place. He raised it and put it quietly to one side.

It was very dark beneath the opening and he flashed the light down once for a brief second. It was long enough to show him that a ladder led from the opening to the floor of the musty, unoccupied room below.

So far, so good!

He whispered to Joe.

"All right. Come ahead."

In the aperture in the roof he could see Joe's form silhouetted, and then his brother scrambled down beside him in the attic.

"I've found a trapdoor," Frank whispered.

"Where does it lead to?"

"There's another room directly below us. It's empty. The workroom must be just below that. But there's a door at the far side of the room, and I think it leads to the stairs that run to the bottom of the mill."

"Shall we go ahead?"

"May as well. We haven't been seen yet. Nor heard."

Frank handed the flashlight to his brother, then groped his way to the trapdoor. He managed to place one foot on the top rung of the ladder beneath the opening.

It held beneath his weight, although the ladder creaked warningly.

Cautiously, step by step, he descended.

There was the utmost need for silence. From the position of the flash of light that he had seen through the crack in the boarded window, he judged that the workroom of the counterfeiters was about midway in the mill, immediately below the deserted room into which he was now descending. The mill widened out toward the bottom, and Frank judged that the locked stone room on the ground floor and the room above were those used by the men.

He reached the bottom of the ladder at last, touching the floor without a sound. He whispered back to Joe, and in a few seconds a faint noise from above told him that his brother was also descending into the dark room.

The rumble of machinery was louder and came from directly beneath his feet. Also he could hear a muffled murmur of voices. He had not been mistaken. The workroom was immediately beneath.

Joe reached the bottom of the ladder in silence. Frank groped for the flashlight. He switched it on.

The room in which they were standing was a low-ceilinged, bare chamber, on the far side of which was a doorway that led to a flight of stairs. Frank stepped cautiously over to the door and peered down the stairs. They led to a landing a short distance below, and continued from there to the bottom of the mill. The room beneath the one in which they were standing evidently opened onto the landing.

Frank made a mental note of all these features so that he would have a good idea of the layout of the building in case it became necessary for them to make a hurried retreat.

He heard a whisper from behind him.

He turned quickly.

Joe was crouching on the floor, peering through a crack in the boards. He motioned to Frank to come over.

# CHAPTER XXIII

## THE ALARM

FRANK crouched on the floor beside his brother.

He switched off the flashlight. The room was in darkness. Immediately he could see a glow of light through one of the cracks in the flooring.

By crouching close to the floor he could see through the cracks into the room beneath.

At the sight he saw he almost gave an exclamation of triumph. There were three men in the room, the three men of the mill—Uncle Dock, his companion, and Markel. They were standing beside a machine that looked like a small printing press. Their sleeves were rolled up and they were wearing inky aprons.

The printing press was rumbling steadily and Markel was feeding it with small sheets of peculiar greenish paper.

But it was what was heaped on a low table beside the press that particularly attracted the attention of the Hardy boys.

189

There they saw neat bundles of crisp, new bills. They were heaped high on the low table, each bundle in a thin, paper wrapper, and their denominations ranged from five to fifty dollars.

"They're printing counterfeit money!" whispered Frank.

Joe nodded. A tingling excitement possessed them. In spite of the fact that they knew the bills were counterfeit there was something fascinating in the sight of those hundreds of crisp, green bills.

Their view of the room was limited, but by moving from side to side they were gradually able to take in all the details of the little chamber. Above the constant rumble of the press they could hear the voices of three men.

"Once we get this shipment sent out we'll be on easy street," said Uncle Dock.

"If we can get it all placed," grumbled Markel.

"We'll get it placed all right," said the other man. "We haven't had any trouble so far. Burgess and his crowd have put over their part of the deal pretty well."

"It'd be better if they'd stay away from Bayport," said Markel. "First thing we know, they'll be figuring the money is coming from here."

"Why should they?" said Uncle Dock.

"It's being sent around to the other towns as well as Bayport."

"That fool Paul Blum mighty near gave the game away."

"He can't say anything. He doesn't know where the stuff is coming from. I think he has an idea we're round the mill, but he isn't sure. He won't give us away."

"Just the same," said Markel, "I'll be relieved when the whole thing is over and we can get out of here. This patent breakfast food story is all right for a while, but country people are too curious. The farmers are talking because we won't do any milling for them."

"Let 'em talk. We'll be out of here by the end of the week. That last photo-engraving you made for us is a good one. It would take an expert to tell it from the original. We'll make fifty thousand dollars from that shipment of tens alone."

"It's good enough," admitted Markel, evidently pleased with the compliment, "but I've said all along that our paper is too thin. It should have just a little more body to it. But it's too hard to imitate. The genuine banknote paper is a bit heavier."

"What's the matter with you to-night, Markel?" asked Uncle Dock. "You have been nervous and jumpy all evening. First of all, you think you see some one sneaking around the mill. Now you're afraid we're all going to be pinched. By the end of the week we'll be out of here and living on the fat of the land. This is the biggest counterfeiting deal that has ever been put across in the United States. I'd imagine you'd be feeling proud of yourself. By the time it is all over we should be worth a quarter of a million dollars each.''

"All the more reason for being careful. You have to watch your step in a game like this.''

"And haven't we watched our step? Who would ever suspect this old mill? Why, there's Hardy, the detective, living right in Bayport. He has never suspected a thing. And the Federal dicks think we have a plant somewhere in the woods back of Barmet village!''

"It was a good idea to take over the mill, I'll admit. But the sooner we're out of here, the better.''

"Well, the last batch of bills will be run off to-night. We'll clear out to-morrow morning and send down for the machinery as soon as we can.''

Frank nudged his brother. So the counterfeiters were planning an early escape!

They peered through the cracks in the floor and watched the three men moving about as the press rumbled and bill after bill was added to the pile on the table.

"Easier way to make money than working,"
remarked Uncle Dock, with a satisfied smile.

"I'm going to take a trip around the world
with my share," said the second man.

"What are you going to do, Markel?"

"I'll follow the horses. I'm going to visit
every race track in America this year. I'll
double my money."

"You'll lose every cent of it."

"No chance."

Uncle Dock smiled.

"Wait and see. Smarter men than you have
lost all their money on the horses."

Frank and Joe had heard enough and had
seen enough to know that there was no further
doubt as to the nature of the activities of the
three men of the mill. They had seen the
counterfeiting plant in operation and from the
conversation of the three men there was no
doubt but that this was the plant that had been
responsible for flooding the East with spurious
bills in the past few weeks.

The counterfeiters were evidently running
off a last shipment of bills before closing up
the plant and moving away. It behooved the
Hardy boys to act quickly.

"Where will we go when we clear out?" they
heard Markel say.

"We'll separate," answered Uncle Dock.
"We'll meet in New York."

"Where?"

"We'll meet Burgess at his apartment. You remember the address don't you?" Uncle Dock gave an address in the Forties, and Frank instantly registered it in his memory. It might come in useful in case the counterfeiters slipped through their hands.

He got up slowly from his cramped position, and Joe followed his example. Frank led the way toward the door that opened on the landing.

"We'd better get out of here," he whispered.

"What will we do?"

"We'll go to Bayport for help. We can't tackle these fellows alone."

"How will we get out? There's no use trying to get out by the roof. We might break our necks trying to reach that tree again."

"We can go down the stairs," said Frank quietly.

"And out the front door?"

"It's probably only bolted on the inside. If we can get past the door of that workroom we should be all right."

"Come on, then."

Frank led the way. He stepped out on the landing. Both boys were wearing light "sneakers" that made little noise.

Step by step, they descended the stairs. Step by step, they drew closer to the landing that led to the counterfeiters' room. They could hear the muffled sound of the printing press and the vague voices of the three men.

They reached the landing at last. A streak of yellow light shone from beneath the door of the workroom. The stairs led on toward the bottom of the mill.

Each lad held his breath as he traversed the dangerous distance to the next flight of stairs. Here, if anywhere, they were in danger of being heard.

But the low voices within the room continued; the steady rumble of the press went on without interruption. Frank gained the top of the steps. Joe followed.

They went slowly down the stairs. Frank could see the dim outlines of the mill machinery in the large room below, with the dark shape of the door in the distance. Once they gained the door they would be comparatively safe.

The thought had hardly crossed his mind when his foot struck suddenly against some solid object.

There was a slight noise, the object moved, then it went clattering down the stairs with an uproar that seemed to awaken the echoes from one end of the mill to the other.

He had kicked over a pail that had been left lying on the steps!

The noise would not be unnoticed—he knew that. With a bound, he had reached the bottom of the steps. There was no time to seek escape by the door, for already he could hear some one running across the floor of the workroom above. They must hide, and hide quickly.

Joe was close behind him.

Frank turned and sped through an open doorway close at hand. The boys found themselves in a gloomy stone room in which several large pieces of machinery could be dimly distinguished in the faint light.

From the floor above they could hear voices. A door opened. Frank glanced back and he could see a beam of light against the wall by the stairs.

"I'm certain I heard a noise!" they heard Markel saying. "I'm going to find out what caused it."

# CHAPTER XXIV

## TRAPPED

THE Hardy boys could see little chance of escape.

Markel was coming down the stairs. They could hear his heavy boots as they clattered on the steps.

Frank glanced around the room. There was one window, but it was boarded up. There was but one door, the one through which they had come.

Markel had reached the foot of the stairs by now. They heard him give a grunt of surprise as he picked up the pail.

"This was what did it," he called back to some one on the landing. "It fell down the stairs."

"Well, what of it?" Uncle Dock called down to him.

"Some one must have knocked it over."

"Couldn't have been any one," sniffed Uncle Dock. "There's nobody around. It's just your nerves."

"Pails don't fall downstairs unless somebody knocks them over," said Markel stubbornly.

"Ask Lester. Perhaps it was him."

They heard Markel go into another room. For a few moments there was silence. Then Markel came out again.

"He's asleep—or shamming. I didn't waken him. But I'm going to take a look around, just the same."

His footsteps drew nearer the room in which the brothers were hiding. Frank sprang lightly in behind the open door, pressing himself close against the wall. Joe wedged in beside him.

Markel came into the room.

He was carrying a flashlight and its beam illuminated the corners of the musty chamber. The Hardy boys waited in suspense. Would he think of looking behind the door?

Suddenly there was a mutter of disgust from Markel and a rustle as something flitted out of a corner.

"Me-e-ow!"

"Only the cat!" grunted Markel.

The animal purred ingratiatingly, but Markel aimed a vicious kick at the cat. It missed its mark, however, and Markel turned and trudged out of the room.

"Find anything?" called Uncle Dock from the top of the stairs.

"It was only the cat," answered Markel sullenly. "The brute must have been prowling around on the stairs and knocked the pail over."

"Well, come back and get to work. I hope you're satisfied now. I knew it must have been something like that."

Markel gave no answer, but went back up the stairs. After a while the door of the workroom banged behind him and soon the roar and rattle of the printing press broke out anew.

Frank took a deep breath.

"That's the closest call I ever went through," he whispered, in relief.

"Let's get out of here. Quick! I'd like to give that cat about a quart of cream for breakfast."

They tiptoed quietly out of the room and made their way to the front door of the mill. It was, as Frank had predicted, bolted on the inside, but he drew the bolt and the door swung slowly open.

Frank placed his fingers on his lips as a sign for silence. To this Joe nodded understandingly.

Then from a distance came an unexpected sound—the mewing of a cat!

Both lads had to grin—indeed, it was all

Joe could do to keep from laughing outright.

They slipped outside, closing the door behind them.

"Now to get back to Bayport," whispered Frank. "We'll have to hurry."

They sped across the grass toward the borders of the dark wood, and not until they had reached its friendly shade did they look behind. The ghostly old mill stood by the gleaming river, dark and sinister in the clear moonlight.

"We'll be back," Joe said, as he glanced back at the mill.

"There is going to be a big surprise for that gang before the night is over."

"I'll say. Let's get started on it."

They ran up through the trees until they reached the deserted road, where they had left their motorcycles. Within a few minutes they were in the saddles and roaring back in the direction of Bayport.

They made the journey at full speed, but at that it was late before the gleaming lights of the city came into view. The motorcycles sped down the shore road on to the concrete boulevards, then raced through the city streets, now almost deserted save for an occasional late trolley or nighthawk taxi.

At length they drew up before the Hardy home and raced up the front walk. They

found their father in the house, sitting up for
them.

"What on earth kept you out so late? Your
mother—" Fenton Hardy began, but Frank
interrupted him.

"We've found the counterfeiters!"

"The what?" demanded Mr. Hardy, in as-
tonishment.

"The counterfeiters. Get some men and we
can catch the whole crowd this very minute."

"Is this right?" asked the detective swiftly.

"We've found their plant. We saw them
making money. We can bring you there right
away. They don't know that we saw them."

"And they're getting ready to leave in the
morning," put in Joe.

"Where are they?" demanded Fenton
Hardy.

"In the old Turner mill on Willow River.
We've just come from there."

Mr. Hardy was a man who wasted little time
once he had grasped the essentials of a situation. Without a word he hurried over to his
study and picked up the telephone. He asked
for a number and, after it was secured, he held
a brief, curt conversation. Then he put down
the telephone and the receiver clicked.

"We'll have a posse out there in half an
hour," he said to his sons. "Three state
troopers and two Secret Service men who

have been working on this case are in town. Will that be enough?"

"There are three in the counterfeiting gang," Frank told him.

"We'll have enough. And now tell me how you found out about the old mill."

Briefly, Frank and Joe told him how their suspicions had first been aroused by the mysterious activities about the mill, how they had visited the place and found that strangers were not welcome, how they had finally resolved to investigate for themselves, and how they had that night gone to the mill and seen the counterfeiting plant in actual operation.

Their story was interrupted by the arrival of an automobile which drew up in front of the Hardy home with a squeal of brakes. A man in uniform stepped out and ran up the walk.

"Here are the officers," said Mr. Hardy. "Come along."

They left the house and met the officer on the steps. Mr. Hardy spoke to him.

"They are at the old Turner mill on Willow River," he said quietly. "I suppose you know how to get there."

"Can't say that I do," said the officer. "Not by car."

"Follow the shore road and then cut in on that deserted loop. It used to run right past the mill before the shore road was built."

The trooper nodded.

"I remember now. The deserted road, eh? We'll get there all right."

"Better leave the car back on the road some distance and go the rest of the way on foot," suggested Frank. "We can sneak up on 'em better that way."

They clambered into the automobile. The other men were broad-shouldered, keen-eyed fellows with determined faces. The moonlight glinted on rifle barrels and revolvers.

Through the cool night sped the automobile, out the shore road, leaving Bayport behind, until at last the car turned off into the deserted road, rocking and bumping to and fro in the ruts.

When they reached the place where Frank and Joe had abandoned the motorcycles earlier in the evening the boys spoke to the driver, whereupon he brought the car to a stop.

They got out and stood in a little group in the moonlit road. Fenton Hardy was in charge of the raid, and he gave his orders quickly and with precision. The men were to follow the road until they reached the meadow between the wood and the mill. The troopers were to deploy out so as to come up in the rear of the mill; the Secret Service men and the others were to take the front way.

They trudged down the road until at last

they stood at the edge of the wood and they
could see the mill below them in the moonlight.
Then the three troopers moved off to the right,
keeping well in the shade, preparatory to cut-
ting down across the meadow toward the back
of the mill.

Fenton Hardy, the two Secret Service men
and the boys walked boldly across the meadow.

They were not seen. There was not a sound
from the mill.

When they reached the front of the building they could see the dark forms of the three
troopers who flitted across the grass and
waited in readiness back of the mill in case any
one should attempt to escape that way.

Mr. Hardy tried the front door. It swung
open. He stepped inside. The Secret Service
men followed. The boys crowded close at their
heels.

"Which room?" whispered the detective.

"At the top of the stairs," Frank told him.

At that moment the door of the workroom
opened and they could see a man run out onto
the landing.

"Who's there?" called out a startled voice.

It was Markel. He was clearly silhouetted
in the light from the workroom.

"The police," answered Mr. Hardy. "Put
up your hands! We have you covered."

In reply, Markel flung himself flat on the

floor, there was a streak of crimson, and a revolver shot roared out. Mr. Hardy and the
Secret Service men had their weapons ready
and they replied with a fusillade of shots.

The light in the room at the head of the
landing had gone out. With a bound, Mr.
Hardy reached the stairs, then raced up the
steps. When he reached the landing, however,
he found that it was deserted. Markel had
escaped the bullets and had crawled back into
the room, for the door was closed.

Fenton Hardy launched himself against the
door of the workroom, but it did not budge.
He could hear sounds of voices, a noise of
banging and of running about in the room beyond.

The Secret Service men and the two boys
reached the landing.

"Break in the door!" snapped Mr. Hardy.

Together they launched themselves against
the door, and there was a splintering sound,
but still the barrier held.

"Again!"

With a concerted rush they plunged forward
once more. The door fell in with a crash.

Fenton Hardy switched on his flashlight, for
the room was in darkness.

There was the printing press, there was the
table with the packages of counterfeit money
—but the counterfeiters were gone. The win-

dow was wide open. They had made their escape that way.

From beneath the window came the sound of rough voices, a shot, a loud yell. Mr. Hardy ran to the window and looked out.

"We got 'em, sir!" called out a voice.

Underneath the willow tree were six figures, and three of them were troopers. Each man held a prisoner. The counterfeiters had been captured.

# CHAPTER XXV

## The Reckoning

WHEN the full story of the activities of the counterfeiters became known next day, Bayport found that the Hardy boys had succeeded in breaking up one of the most dangerous bands that had ever baffled the Federal authorities.

After the capture of Uncle Dock and his associates, Fenton Hardy and the Secret Service men had wasted no time. Frank had remembered the New York address of the mysterious Burgess, that he had heard Uncle Dock mention, and a telegram to the New York police resulted in the arrest of this man, who turned out to be the brains of the gang, the man who had arranged for the distribution of the spurious bills. The crooks in Barmet village, and the rascally woman in black were also apprehended.

"The machinery in the mill," Mr. Hardy told his sons, "was the most complete and efficient they could obtain. Markel, it seems,

was at one time an expert photo-engraver. He
furnished the engravings that enabled them to
make such an excellent imitation of United
States currency, while Uncle Dock and the
other man helped him turn out the bills.
Burgess saw to it that they got the proper
paper and also planned the distribution. There
were enough bad bills lying on the table when
we raided the place to have netted them almost
half a million dollars between them.''

Thanks to the quick work of the officers, not
one member of the gang had escaped. In
Burgess' rooms had been found a notebook
containing the names and addresses of the
agents he had working for him, distributing
the counterfeit money throughout the country,
and by the next day every man had been apprehended.

The two Secret Service men who had aided
in the final round-up of the counterfeiters at
the old mill called personally at the Hardy
home next day to congratulate the boys.

''We've been working around here for almost a week trying to get the goods on these
men,'' said one, ''but never once did we think
of the old mill. What made you suspicious of
that place?''

Frank told him how they had first learned
that strangers had taken over the mill and told
of their first visit to the place.

"To tell the truth," he said, "my first suspicions were when Uncle Dock offered to give us a reward for helping save Lester from the river. He took two five dollar bills from his pocket and offered them to us. Then the other man snatched them from him, turned around, and later offered them to us again."

The Secret Service man smiled.

"Uncle Dock offered you two counterfeit bills and the other man was afraid they would be detected and that you would know where they came from."

"I suppose that was his idea. But it made me suspicious. After that, Joe and I kept watching the place and as everything seemed to indicate that something suspicious was going on at the mill we made up our mind to pay them a visit."

"And a very lucky thing it was that you did. It was a smart piece of work and I want to assure you that the Government won't forget it."

The Government did not forget it. Before the month was out, the Hardy boys had received a check for one thousand dollars as a reward for the part they had played in the capture of the counterfeiters.

"Enough money," Chet Morton said when he heard of it, "to buy gas for the motorboat for a couple of years, anyway."

As for Uncle Dock and his gang, they were all sentenced to long terms of imprisonment. Frank and Joe made particular inquiries about Lester and they asked their father to see to it that the boy was well taken care of. The result of Mr. Hardy's efforts in Lester's behalf was the discovery that "Uncle Dock" was not the boy's uncle at all, but a rascally impostor who had made claim for the lad at an orphan asylum and who had planned to bring him up in a life of crime.

A well-to-do citizen of Bayport, who heard of the case, offered to give Lester a home and see that he was sent to school. The boy was accordingly assured of a brighter future than had confronted him while he was with Uncle Dock, and no one was more pleased than the Hardy boys.

"We'll take you out with us in the motor-boat, Lester," they told him.

"Will you?" he asked, his face lighting up with pleasure.

"Sure—you're one of the gang now."

"And will you take me with you when you go detectiving?"

"When we go what?" exclaimed Joe.

"When you go detectiving."

The Hardy boys laughed.

"Oh, you mean when we're trying to be detectives. We'll see, Lester. But the chances are we won't have a chance to be detectives for a long while now. Counterfeiters don't start operating around Bayport every day, you know.''

''And it's a good thing they don't,'' Joe added.

But the Hardy boys were destined to have other adventures in which they were to have opportunities of displaying their ability as detectives quite as timely as those which had fallen to their lot in the affair of the old mill. What some of these happenings were will be related in the next volume, called, ''The Hardy Boys: The Missing Chums.''

When they received their check which was the reward from the Government for their clever work in running the counterfeiters to earth, they were accompanied to the bank by Chet Morton and Lester, Jerry Gilroy and Phil Cohen, Tony Prito and Biff Hooper, for the Hardy boys had promised to celebrate by treating their friends to ice-cream, to be followed by a motorboat race, wherein Tony, in the *Napoli,* was going to make a second attempt to beat the *Sleuth.*

''I guess ten dollars will cover it,'' said Frank, as he handed the check over to the cashier. ''We can buy gas with the money that's left over.''

''And you want to deposit nine hundred and ninety dollars?''

"Yes."

The cashier handed over two five dollar bills. Chet Morton seized one, bit it, gazed reflectively at the ceiling for a moment, then gave it back to Frank.

"I guess it's good," he said. "There's so much counterfeit money going around, these days, that one can't be too careful."

**THE END**

# This Isn't All!

Would you like to know what became of the good friends you have made in this book?

Would you like to read other stories continuing their adventures and experiences, or other books quite as entertaining by the same author?

On the *reverse side* of the wrapper which comes with this book, you will find a wonderful list of stories which you can buy at the same store where you got this book.

## Don't throw away the Wrapper

*Use it as a handy catalog of the books you want some day to have. But in case you do mislay it, write to the Publishers for a complete catalog.*

# THE TOM SWIFT SERIES
## By VICTOR APPLETON

**Uniform Style of Binding.    Individual Colored Wrappers. Every Volume Complete in Itself.**

Every boy possesses some form of inventive genius. Tom Swift is a bright, ingenious boy and his inventions and adventures make the most interesting kind of reading.

TOM SWIFT AND HIS MOTOR CYCLE
TOM SWIFT AND HIS MOTOR BOAT
TOM SWIFT AND HIS AIRSHIP
TOM SWIFT AND HIS SUBMARINE BOAT
TOM SWIFT AND HIS ELECTRIC RUNABOUT
TOM SWIFT AND HIS WIRELESS MESSAGE
TOM SWIFT AMONG THE DIAMOND MAKERS
TOM SWIFT IN THE CAVES OF ICE
TOM SWIFT AND HIS SKY RACER
TOM SWIFT AND HIS ELECTRIC RIFLE
TOM SWIFT IN THE CITY OF GOLD
TOM SWIFT AND HIS AIR GLIDER
TOM SWIFT IN CAPTIVITY
TOM SWIFT AND HIS WIZARD CAMERA
TOM SWIFT AND HIS GREAT SEARCHLIGHT
TOM SWIFT AND HIS GIANT CANNON
TOM SWIFT AND HIS PHOTO TELEPHONE
TOM SWIFT AND HIS AERIAL WARSHIP
TOM SWIFT AND HIS BIG TUNNEL
TOM SWIFT IN THE LAND OF WONDERS
TOM SWIFT AND HIS WAR TANK
TOM SWIFT AND HIS AIR SCOUT
TOM SWIFT AND HIS UNDERSEA SEARCH
TOM SWIFT AMONG THE FIRE FIGHTERS
TOM SWIFT AND HIS ELECTRIC LOCOMOTIVE
TOM SWIFT AND HIS FLYING BOAT
TOM SWIFT AND HIS GREAT OIL GUSHER
TOM SWIFT AND HIS CHEST OF SECRETS
TOM SWIFT AND HIS AIRLINE EXPRESS

GROSSET & DUNLAP,    PUBLISHERS,    NEW YORK

# THE DON STURDY SERIES

## By VICTOR APPLETON

Individual Colored Wrappers and Text Illustrations by
WALTER S. ROGERS
Every Volume Complete in Itself.

In company with his uncles, one a mighty hunter and the other a noted scientist, Don Sturdy travels far and wide, gaining much useful knowledge and meeting many thrilling adventures.

### DON STURDY ON THE DESERT OF MYSTERY;

An engrossing tale of the Sahara Desert, of encounters with wild animals and crafty Arabs.

### DON STURDY WITH THE BIG SNAKE HUNTERS;

Don's uncle, the hunter, took an order for some of the biggest snakes to be found in South America—to be delivered alive!

### DON STURDY IN THE TOMBS OF GOLD;

A fascinating tale of exploration and adventure in the Valley of Kings in Egypt.

### DON STURDY ACROSS THE NORTH POLE;

A great polar blizzard nearly wrecks the airship of the explorers.

### DON STURDY IN THE LAND OF VOLCANOES;

An absorbing tale of adventures among the volcanoes of Alaska.

### DON STURDY IN THE PORT OF LOST SHIPS;

This story is just full of exciting and fearful experiences on the sea.

### DON STURDY AMONG THE GORILLAS;

A thrilling story of adventure in darkest Africa. Don is carried over a mighty waterfall into the heart of gorilla land.

GROSSET & DUNLAP, *Publishers,* NEW YORK

# THE RADIO BOYS SERIES

(Trademark Registered)

## By ALLEN CHAPMAN

Author of the "Railroad Series," Etc.

**Individual Colored Wrappers. Illustrated.
Every Volume Complete in Itself.**

A new series for boys giving full details of radio work, both in sending and receiving—telling how small and large amateur sets can be made and operated, and how some boys got a lot of fun and adventure out of what they did. Each volume from first to last is so thoroughly fascinating, so strictly up-to-date and accurate, we feel sure all lads will peruse them with great delight.

Each volume has a Foreword by Jack Binns, the well-known radio expert.

THE RADIO BOYS' FIRST WIRELESS

THE RADIO BOYS AT OCEAN POINT

THE RADIO BOYS AT THE SENDING
STATION

THE RADIO BOYS AT MOUNTAIN PASS

THE RADIO BOYS TRAILING A VOICE

THE RADIO BOYS WITH THE FOREST
RANGERS

THE RADIO BOYS WITH THE ICEBERG
PATROL

THE RADIO BOYS WITH THE FLOOD
FIGHTERS

THE RADIO BOYS ON SIGNAL ISLAND

THE RADIO BOYS IN GOLD VALLEY

GROSSET & DUNLAP, *Publishers,* NEW YORK

# GARRY GRAYSON FOOTBALL STORIES

## By ELMER A. DAWSON

**Individual Colored Wrappers and Illustrations by
WALTER S. ROGERS
Every Volume Complete in Itself**

Football followers all over the country will hail with delight this new and thoroughly up-to-date line of gridiron tales.

Garry Grayson is a football fan, first, last, and all the time. But more than that, he is a wideawake American boy with a "gang" of chums almost as wideawake as himself.

How Garry organized the first football eleven his grammar school had, how he later played on the High School team, and what he did on the Prep School gridiron and elsewhere, is told in a manner to please all readers and especially those interested in watching a rapid forward pass, a plucky tackle, or a hot run for a touchdown.

Good, clean football at its best—and in addition, rattling stories of mystery and schoolboy rivalries.

GARRY GRAYSON'S HILL STREET ELEVEN;
   or, The Football Boys of Lenox.

GARRY GRAYSON AT LENOX HIGH; or, The
   Champions of the Football League.

GARRY GRAYSON'S FOOTBALL RIVALS; or,
   The Secret of the Stolen Signals.

GARRY GRAYSON SHOWING HIS SPEED; or,
   A Daring Run on the Gridiron.

GARRY GRAYSON AT STANLEY PREP; or, The
   Football Rivals of Riverview.

GROSSET & DUNLAP, *Publishers,* NEW YORK

# WESTERN STORIES FOR BOYS
## By JAMES CODY FERRIS

**Individual Colored Wrappers and Illustrations by
WALTER S. ROGERS
Each Volume Complete in Itself.**

Thrilling tales of the great west, told primarily for boys but which will be read by all who love mystery, rapid action, and adventures in the great open spaces.

The Manley Boys, Roy and Teddy, are the sons of an old ranchman, the owner of many thousands of heads of cattle. The lads know how to ride, how to shoot, and how to take care of themselves under any and all circumstances.

The cowboys of the X Bar X Ranch are real cowboys, on the job when required but full of fun and daring---a bunch any reader will be delighted to know

THE X BAR X BOYS ON THE RANCH

THE X BAR X BOYS IN THUNDER CANYON

THE X BAR X BOYS ON WHIRLPOOL RIVER

THE X BAR X BOYS ON BIG BISON TRAIL

THE X BAR X BOYS AT THE ROUND-UP

GROSSET & DUNLAP, *Publishers*, NEW YORK